FINAL
CUT

FINAL CUT

Arthur Winfield Knight

MILVERSTEAD PUBLISHING

Philadelphia

Thanks to my wife Kit, who let me base Kathleen's entries on a journal she kept while pregnant

Milverstead Publishing LLC
31 Rampart Drive
Wayne, PA 19087
(888)667-3981

Visit us on the web!

www.milversteadpublishing.com

For Bill Pronzini and Marcia Muller,
with thanks for all the kind words

She came hang gliding, nude, over Topaz Lake, a hundred feet or so above the water. She was delicate and white, and her long blonde hair glistened in the sunlight. Cloud shadows spread out like birthmarks on the speckled yellow hills behind her. The leaves on the trees along the lake were chartreuse, fluttering out over the white-capped water. A light wind blew. People in small boats looked up, as if they couldn't believe what they were seeing.

Kathleen said, "You know you're in Nevada. Anything goes," but the lake crossed the state line into California. Trout weighing as much as eight pounds had been caught there.

It was early April, but there was still snow on the southern peaks. The lake was just over five thousand feet high, and it was built by the Army Corp of Engineers in 1923. Prior to that the land consisted of a dry lake bed known as Alkali Lake, but the name was changed because alkali had a bad connotation. People imagined a place that re-sembled The Great Salt Lake, a place of hydroxides and ammonium, when the opposite was true. You could fish or swim or boat in Topaz Lake, and the surrounding Pine Nut Mountains rose up around it like slightly scorched marshmallows during the summer.

A soft woolen moon was barely visible in the noon sky when Sam and Kathleen went into the lodge to have lunch. Their waitress' chin stuck in her neck and she breathed like someone dying of emphy-sema. It made Sam glad he'd quit smoking.

Kathleen ordered Bubba's Fried Bologna Sandwich, and Sam or-dered a pastrami sandwich with coleslaw dressing, while they watched a lone pelican in the water below them. It kept bobbing its head below the surface of the lake and they simultaneously said, "It must be a poet," because it was a standing joke between them.

Poets could be a solitary, surly drunken bunch, so they were often loners. Kathleen knew several when Sam had met her and she was a student at the University of California in Davis.

Kathleen's hair was the color of sunburnt grasses in the dazzling light that came through the window next to their booth.

Sam asked the waitress if she knew how long the lake was when she came with their sandwiches and she said, "I have no idea." No one seemed to know. Not the cashier. Not the guy who sold fishing licenses at the general store. Not the gas station attendant dumping windshield water that glistened like dark stars across the greasy pavement.

They watched a dog, the color of late-winter-afternoon shadows on crusted snow, sniffing at a bush, then they went down the path to the water's edge.

An Indian lady with five chins and a dog hummed "What a Friend We Have in Jesus," and the light came through the trees and turned the dust to gold. The blue-green water shimmered. Sam was twenty-five years older than Kathleen, and their marriage seemed inexplicable at times. They held hands, walking along the lake. The flashes of sweet light, the love, the kindness of hope would never die. Sam had been a cynic when they met.

Kathleen said, "We're going to have a baby."

They were married on a windy afternoon in Carson City. It was mid-October, but the leaves were already changing color. The yellow aspens trembled in the wind as they came down the courthouse steps. Sam held Kathleen's hand, steadying her, because she'd been hit by a car when she was eighteen, and had been in a coma for nine weeks.

They'd stood in line, waiting to apply for their marriage license, next to some paint cans in the hall. The fumes were intoxicating. The couple behind them had acted as their witnesses.

The judge who'd married them never smiled, but he probably married hundreds of couples a day. His job was probably as exciting as one on an assembly line at General Motors.

Kathleen's parents had been invited, but they hated Sam. They thought he'd ruined her first marriage, but it had been ruined before he'd met her. They thought he was too old for her, and Kathleen's mother called him a three time loser, although he'd only been divorced twice. His third wife, Sara, had died when she was thirty. Neither of Kathleen's parents had liked the movies he'd made. They thought they were too violent, obscene, but a lot of people did. Some of his critics called him Bloody Sam, but they didn't know what they were talking about.

They went into a small bar and ordered a bottle of chardonnay. There was a huge framed color photograph of John Wayne that was illuminated by a light attached to the bottom of the frame, a black and white drawing of the Duke and a statue of him that was probably a foot high on a shelf behind the bar. It could have been a cloister.

Sam told the barmaid, "Someone must like John Wayne," and she said, "Doesn't everyone?"

Sam didn't say anything because there was no point in hurting her feelings, but he and Kathleen sat at a window table with their backs to the Duke.

The sky was the color of bruised roses.

"To us," Kathleen said. "It wasn't always easy."

"I wouldn't have it any other way."

"Suppose they came back," Sam said. "Suppose Doc and Carol ran out of money in Mexico, so they show up in Nevada, looking for another bank to rob. It might make a good film."

He and Kathleen sat across the table from each other in their kitchen in Sacramento. Home again, where the wild turkeys paraded in the rain, and smoke curdled around the neon lights when it was smoggy, like milk poured into vinegar.

Doc had been played by Steve McQueen and Carol had been played by Ali MacGraw in a film Sam had directed. Sam remembered picking her up with Steve when she'd arrived in Texas for location work. Steve was recently divorced and Ali had a one year old son, but Ali and Steve were fucking minutes after they'd met. It was an old story in Hollywood.

Steve had told Ali, "Baby, you look great in jeans and a T-shirt," but he could be cruel, too. Intelligent people intimidated him, especially women. Sam remembered Steve telling Ali, "You have a great ass, but you better start working out now, because I don't want to wake up one day with a woman who's got an ass like a seventy-year-old Japanese soldier."

When the picture wrapped, Ali had told Sam, "I was photographed ten thousand times being charming and loving to everyone, including my husband, when the real story was adultery in Texas. I felt like a piece of garbage," but she was a sensitive, beautiful woman. Better than McQueen deserved. That, too, was an old story in Hollywood.

He'd had two kids, Sam Jr. and Ellie, with his first wife, and another son, Christopher, with his second, but that was all Sam knew about his children, their names, and he suspected they despised him. He wouldn't blame them if they did. He was too busy being famous or whoring or getting drunk with his cronies to be a father. Edie and Karen had done all the work.

Sam remembered watching some children push an inflatable rubber raft into a river when he and Sara were in South Dakota. The tires of the Cadillac reverberated on the wooden planks of the bridge while the kids screamed and splashed below. They were wet and dirty and probably happier than most people.

Sara said, "Given everything, I'm glad we never had any kids, aren't you?"

"Yeah, it's a blessing," Sam said, but he was lying.

This time he was going to get it right.

Kathleen said, "I remember going to my classes when it was raining. I had a blue plastic raincoat and a plastic hat that I could stuff into my purse. I already knew the marriage was over, but I had no idea what I was going to do. Someone told me I looked like the girl on the box of salt, holding the umbrella, *when it rains, it pours*, but my umbrella was broken.

"Later, a friend bought me a small silver necklace in the shape of a girl holding an umbrella, but he had a jeweler drill a hole in the umbrella because he thought I was the saddest person on campus."

"Maybe you were," Sam said.

They followed the Ford pickup to the Indian cemetery in Schurz. The sun burnt a purple hole through the center of a rain cloud above the mountains in the distance, but it almost never rained in Nevada. That would help to make it a good place to shoot, although Sam remembered it had rained for more than a week when he'd shot one of his films here. Overhead, jet trails feathered out like plumes against an incredibly blue sky, and the clouds spun out like Angel Hair.

Some of the wooden crosses were so old they'd disintegrated, and whatever names or dates were inscribed on them were lost long ago. Some of the graves were marked with Mason Jars instead of headstones or crosses, and the jars were filled with fake sun-bleached flowers, but everything was diffused by dust. Entering the cemetery was like entering a faded postcard of Americana.

The ghosts of dandelions blew through the air as they walked toward the grave of the Paiute prophet. White men called him Jack Wilson, but he was known as Wovoka to the Indians. Five abalone shells were on his grave, although they were easily two hundred miles from the nearest ocean. Perhaps the shells had some significance, but Sam had no idea what it might be. Had no idea why there were quarters and beads and a soft coin purse resting on his grave, either.

The headstone read:

WOVOKA

1858 – 1932

FOUNDER OF THE GHOST DANCE, HIS TEACHINGS
OF HOPE, GOOD WILL AND PROMISE OF LIFE
AFTER DEATH WILL LIVE AS LONG AS MAN
INHABITS THIS EARTH.

As a young man, Wovoka had a vision of the western tribes living in harmony with each other and the white man, but it was a vision that went sour when 180 Sioux men, women and children were slaughtered by the cavalry at Wounded Knee, South Dakota in December 1890, because Colonel James Forsyth thought the dance was a preparation for war. It was the last major engagement between the soldiers and the Indians, so Wovoka's vision wasn't entirely in vain.

Indians from the western tribes sought help from Wovoka, who lived in the nearby Mason Valley, during the remainder of his life, believing he was capable of performing miracles. It was said he'd made ice fall from the sky during one summer, and many believed he had the capacity to make it rain. Many also believed he was bullet proof, particularly after he'd danced, which probably had something to do with the tragedy at Wounded Knee.

Wovoka told cowboy movie star Tim McCoy, "I'm never going to die," but of course he did. When death came, his wife went into the streets ringing a bell, the high plains night sky berserk with stars, a lantern lighting her way, the edges of its flame spread out like a butterfly's wings.

A small hurricane of dust surrounded them as they left the cemetery, and the sand was like shattered ivory. They walked out into loneliness, the wind tearing at them. Sam remembered someone saying, "If the soft falling away of the afternoon is all there is, it is nearly enough." He wasn't sure what it meant, but it somehow seemed appropriate as they made their way back to the Cadillac. They drove off into a wall of brilliance, the sunlight banging down onto the car.

They stopped for a drink at Casino West in Yerington, a few miles from the Indian cemetery, because Kathleen was tired, thirsty and hungry. Someone who looked like Cesar Romero sat next to her. He was drinking a draft beer and dropping quarters into the poker machine that was built into the bar. Sam was tempted to say, "I thought you were great as the Cisco Kid," but he couldn't imagine why Romero would be in rural Nevada. But everyone had to be someplace.

Cesar stopped to sip his beer, looking at Kathleen, and said, "This town used to be wild. There were two saloons when the town was founded in the 1860s. One was famous for serving whiskey that was so bad people said it was poison, but their accents made it sound like pizen. The saloon was made of some thatched willows so the local ranchers called it The Switch, and the town got to be known as Pizen Switch, but that didn't sound respectable so it got changed," then he dropped some more quarters into the slot.

Someone sitting across the bar was talking to himself. He was probably ten years younger than Sam, but he had gray hair. He needed a shave, a clean shirt, a shot of Scope, a new life. He might have been a beatnik. He said, loudly, "I do not glum my days away." Everyone avoided looking at him.

Sam and Kathleen got up to go into the restaurant. As they were waiting to be seated, a tall man with thinning silver hair came toward them. His shoulders were slightly slumped. He put his hand out as he approached them and said, "I'm Bob, I'm 93," but kept walking.

Sam said, "I kind of like this place."

"Let's hear it for the crabby people," Kathleen said.

He was sweating when he awakened. For a moment, Sam didn't know where he was, then he remembered, but he touched Kathleen, lying next to him, to be certain. He'd been in too many rooms with too many women who had left him, one way or another. Sara had died.

Sam remembered one room in particular. He'd listened to a Big Ben clock on the bureau next to the bed, lying beside a woman whose name he couldn't remember in Mexico. He'd been shooting an epic Civil War film, but everything had gone wrong. He would have been fired if the star hadn't said he'd give up his salary if Sam could finish the picture. The star was bluffing, but the studio wasn't. The film had been a paralyzed epic.

Sam told the woman, "Listen, the clock is going Humpty, Humpty, Dumpty, Dumpty, Dumpty," but she couldn't speak English. Sam knew it would take more than all the king's men and all the king's horses to get his life on track again, but he'd rolled over and gone back to sleep.

This time, he held on to Kathleen.

"You take the top," Sam said.

It was still dark, but Sam knew she was awake. Her breathing had changed.

"Why?"

"Because of the baby."

"She's months away." Kathleen was sure the baby would be a girl. "You don't have to worry."

"You *always* have to worry," Sam said.

He may not have learned much in 53 years, but that was one thing he was absolutely sure of.

The morning light in the high plains was so startling in its brilliance and clarity that it was like driving through a diamond, the sun glittering on the rivers, blue skies above. The top down on the Cadillac. They passed huge herds of grazing cattle, watching them behind dark glasses.

Wild horses still ran through parts of the area. The buffalo were gone, but it was easy to imagine them roaming the valley. The largest onion producing farm in the world was here. Someone said the air was so pungent you could imagine nothing better than a hamburger smothered with onions when they were ripening in the fall.

They turned off the highway when they saw a sign directing them to Fort Churchill, because Kathleen remembered an episode of *Bonanza* where Ben Cartwright and Little Joe had gone there to buy horses from the cavalry. Sam remembered Tex Ritter singing about Pony Bob, an Express rider who'd pass by the fort, but the song had probably been popular before Kathleen was born.

It was difficult to imagine life at the fort then: the soldiers rising in the faded light of dawn, their days filled with relentless routine and sad songs. Possibly, someone played a harmonica in the heart-stopping blue twilight that covered the high desert. Sam could imagine the moon low on the horizon, veiled with brown dust. Each sunrise must have come to the troops as a testimony to personal failure, something Sam knew too well, far away from home, far away from their loved ones, far away from any form of civilization.

The adobe had crumbled, falling away in patches that resembled undiscovered countries, and no birds sang although they had to be there someplace among the trees that bordered the Carson River. There were scrub jays, robins, hummingbirds and woodpeckers, according to signs posted along a path, but Sam could only hear the wind in the dying dogwoods.

It was the kind of country he'd spent his summers in when he was a child, and he loved it.

He said, "I always wondered why anyone would live any place other than California, but it isn't the same place I grew up in. Everything's been paved over." His eyes watered. "Maybe it's time to go."

Kathleen looked out across the crumbling ruins, as if she expected to see Ben or Little Joe come riding toward them, and looked disappointed when she didn't. "Everything changes."

"I know that, but I don't have to like it," Sam said.

I got a gift in the mail today. The outside of the box told me it was a free gift for Mrs. Sam Bonner and her baby. A tiny pink box of Dreft clothes detergent tumbled out when I unwrapped the package. I smiled and put it in the bag with the box of newborn Pampers we bought last night.

People ask what I want, a boy or a girl. I've always disliked that question, since you don't have a choice. Then they answer their own question, saying, "It doesn't matter so long as it's healthy, right?" Then they smile idiotically. I just sigh. "We don't have any preference, as long as the baby has character."

Years ago, someone said all babies look like Winston Churchill without a cigar. I had to agree, although I've seen a few infants with a wiser, more knowing look to them; that's what I want for our baby.

Buying the box of 30 Pampers last night was strange. It was the first time either of us ever bought a diaper, even though Sam has three kids, and there were directions for putting one on and disposing of it once it was soiled on the outside of the box. I'd changed diapers, a few times, when I was a baby sitter, so I had a general idea of the process. But the explicit directions were comforting.

We sent a friend of ours a birthday card, signing it, "Love, Kathleen and Sam and the one who walks within." It was a phrase someone Sam worked with had used. We liked the poetic sound of it, and it was perfect for Warner, one of the most romantic people we know. I sent him the blue garter I wore the day Sam and I got married.

Warner has eyes like Bela Lugosi in those old Dracula movies, and he's been a heroin addict for 20 years. Now he's on methadone, although he prefers heroin. But it's expensive, illegal and you can't regulate its use. As Warner puts it, "You're shooting up more and more, then, suddenly, you're dead.

My parents would hate him.

Kathleen almost always took the top now when they made love. It wasn't just that she was pregnant. She said she felt more in control of things when they made love that way, more confident. Sam wondered if that's where the phrase "being on top of it" originated.

McQueen had been drunk. He'd spent the day in a Mexican whorehouse, drinking beer all afternoon because he claimed you couldn't get drunk on beer, but he was in no shape to drive when they left the whorehouse. Every *puta* in the place had wanted his autograph. They called him Senor Bullitt because they'd all seen the movie.

Steve wouldn't let Sam take the wheel. It was a matter of pride with him. He was the greatest driver in the world, the greatest stud, the greatest actor. No one made more money than he did. He could be tiring.

He drove a Jaguar, even though they were famous for their faulty electrical systems. He told Sam he liked the way the car handled. At least once a week, he'd press the high beam switch and the lights would short out, but he could reach under the dash and change the fuse in a matter of seconds, even when he was drunk, so he never panicked when it happened.

He was hitting 90 on a darkened highway, heading back to Texas. The top was down because the heat was oppressive, even at midnight, and huge bugs splattered against the windshield. Steve lit a cigarette with his Zippo, hitting the high beam switch when the highway turned to gravel, rocks pinging against the undercarriage. The lights went out and Sam could feel the car swerve, but Steve was laughing, "Not to worry my friend, not to worry, I can handle anything," as they careened down the dark road.

Sam never rode with him again.

Sometimes the sky looked as if someone had pasted ancient, faded pages of the *Sacramento Bee* over the sun, so the light barely filtered through the dust and paper, and people who had problems breathing stayed inside. It seemed as if there were no dawns or sunsets on those days, and it was easy to imagine the sky dissolved somewhere above the State Capitol.

Sometimes, when you approached Sacramento the city seemed like a dream materializing out of the smog, but there were nights when the Delta Breeze came up, blowing across the rice paddies, over the city, and the sky darkened, softening, until it looked like blue blotter paper. But when the wind stopped, the sounds of the city were so strong they could rattle the Venetian blinds in a room that was nearly soundproof.

"We need to get out of here," Sam said.

Women's Lib made sense to me when I was in college. I was lost in my marriage, floundering, and I wanted stability. Since Clark was making a career of the Air Force, I couldn't see any stability in my future. Clark offered suggestions, "Have a baby, it'll keep you busy," "Learn to sew, like my mother," but they were by mail, since he was on a tour of duty in Turkey, and weren't much consolation anyway.

I thought you were supposed to hear angels singing or to feel the earth move when you made love, but I felt… nothing. It was as if there were rocks in our bed. I knew Clark wouldn't do anything to improve our sex life, so I did. I thought I'd find the missing X in sex and teach it to Clark, saving my marriage.

Saving my marriage???

It's been raining all afternoon, one of those sepia tone days when petals lay in uneven circles under the ravaged trees and things are reflections of themselves.

Sam brought me a single, red sweetheart rose and a bottle of champagne, which we drank, and the day didn't seem quite so drab.

Thank you for the rose, darling.

The wind rippled the water as the boat took them out onto Walker Lake. On their way there, they'd passed huge stacks of baled hay covered with blue and white tarps that flapped liked giant kites ready to be blown into the heavens. Sam wondered how it would look on film, wondered why Doc and Carol would come here. Maybe they'd case the bank in Hawthorne. It was only a few miles away.

The wind blew enormous saucer shaped clouds across the sky, and there were yellow signs with pictures of big horn sheep on them. Sometimes the sheep would come down from the mountains.

It was probably 60 degrees along the shore, but there was still snow on Mt. Grant, over fourteen thousand feet high, in the distance. It reminded Sam of the snow-crusted peak you saw at the beginning of a Paramount Picture.

Sam said, "I never thought I'd be looking for loons. I'm not even sure I knew what a loon was until now." They were black duck-like birds with white feathers on their backs and breasts, and they were known for their strange cries. They couldn't walk on land, even though they had webbed feet.

Kathleen asked the game warden piloting the boat, "Why are crazy people called loons?" but he didn't know. He did say the number of loons was decreasing each year because the lake was gradually becoming more saline so there were fewer fish for the birds to feed on. Sam listened to his explanation, although he was more interested in how things felt than facts.

Someone from Holland had told Sam, "The poetry of facts is the poetry of the American soul," but he didn't believe that.

The game warden said various cultures had various myths about loons. Some believed newborn babies who were wiped with the skins of loons were assured health and long life, and some believed loons were sacred and wouldn't even mention their names. Others believed our souls would be wing-shaped if we could see them, but Sam wasn't interested in souls.

He was interested in what he could see. You couldn't put souls on film.

The game warden kept scanning the lake with binoculars, his eyes shaded by a baseball cap with the name Mike on it and wire rimmed dark glasses. The lake was a luminous green, due to the salt and algae. The water level subsided a little more each year. There were no loons in sight.

Mike said, "Maybe our names are written in water and one day the water just dries up," which seemed very philosophical coming from a game warden, then he turned the boat around, the wind chopping the waves, and they headed back toward shore.

I called my parents on Christmas Day. Sam and I were staying at the Peppermill in Reno, and it had been less than a week since I'd left Clark. My dad answered the phone, but wouldn't say anything when he recognized my voice. He called my mother, handing the phone to her. The first thing she said was, "Your husband is here."

I said, "Clark and I are separated. It's over."

I could picture him sitting next to my parents' artificial tree, drinking Pepsi, watching a Tarzan rerun on TV.

"He wants to talk to you."

"I don't want to talk to him." Sam was lying on the bed next to me. "I don't have anything to say."

Mom was convinced Sam would leave me in a couple of years, finding another, younger woman, but she believed what she needed to believe. I'd told her I was so miserable before I'd left Clark that I had suicidal feelings and the danger was real. But even my psychoanalyst couldn't convince her.

I said, "We'll talk later. I just wanted to say Merry Christmas," then I hung up and hugged Sam.

Sam wondered who he'd cast as Doc if he made a sequel to *The Heist*. Steve had just turned 42 when they'd begun shooting in April of '72, but he'd looked at least five years younger. Steve had been 48 when he made *An Enemy of the People* last year, but he was bloated and looked ten years older than he was and Sam heard he'd lost interest in the little things he'd savored: a cold beer, racing motorcycles, tacos with lots of hot sauce.

Steve's first wife, Neile, had told Sam that Steve had a deep-seated fear of homosexuality, but she might just have been getting back at Steve for all the years he'd cheated on her.

The opening scenes in *The Heist* were shot in San Marcos, a small town halfway between San Antonio and Austin, and the first day of rehearsal took place in the conference room of a local bank.

Sam believed Doc wanted to pull one last job so he and Carol would have enough money to stay together without having to rob another bank.

Steve said, "Doc wants to get laid, but he doesn't give a damn about Carol. He feels she's let him down by having an affair to get him out of jail, and he'd never been a one-woman man. Not knowing what love is, he can't give it," but Steve could have been talking about himself or Sam, at the time, or almost anyone in Hollywood.

Steve, Ali and Sam had been drinking champagne all afternoon because it was Sam's birthday, but the argument about Doc's character had finally become so violent Steve hurled the last full magnum at Sam's head. He'd managed to duck, but the bottle knocked the plaster out of the wall.

The three of them stood there, shaking, until Steve finally said, "Happy birthday, you son of a bitch," and left the room.

Ali later told a reporter, "I spent three of the most mind-blowing months of my life making that picture, just in terms of survival."

Sam believed it was a miracle any of them had survived.

A convict wearing a uniform with black and white stripes was raking leaves in front of the Lyon County Courthouse in Yerington. Sam thought uniforms like that had disappeared sometime during the 30s, so the convict didn't seem quite real.

Sam had made a point of driving up Main Street, veering off from the highway as they'd headed home from Walker Lake, but he wasn't sure why.

The convict was talking to someone and the two of them stood next to a huge stone tablet with the Ten Commandments engraved on it.

Sam said, "I thought it was illegal to have religious icons in front of public buildings."

"They call this God's Country for a reason," Kathleen said.

Someone who must have been 80 told them there were six whorehouses in Lyon County but only four stoplights when they'd stopped for a drink at Casino West. The old guy had talked about the need for senor citizens to have a healthy sex life and wondered if he could set up a brothel for the aged that would qualify for Medicare reimbursement. Sam doubted it, but anything seemed possible in Nevada.

They headed west on Highway 50 when they reached Silver Springs. They drove through Dayton, where part of *The Misfits* with Marilyn Monroe and Clark Gable had been shot. Then they passed a chocolate factory on the right and three brothels on the left. Prostitution was legal in some counties in Nevada.

Kathleen said, "You certainly know what's important here, and it isn't chocolate."

Marshall Owens is the only person I know who calls Sam "my dear." They'd worked together in Hollywood, where Marshall had been an administrator of some sort, but he'd moved to what he referred to as The

City, as if San Francisco were the only one in the world. Maybe, to him, it is.

He said he had three friends who were doctors at the hospital where he worked. One was black, one was Jewish and the other was Japanese. They were all complaining about being discriminated against as minorities while they were waiting for an elevator. Marshall began to laugh because they were all earning more than a hundred thousand dollars a year.

"Who can be more of a minority than us?" he'd asked. "A nigger, a kike, a jap and a cock-sucker."

Marshall had put on a red kimono and served us coffee from a silver pot, prancing around the room on his toes. He'd been a ballet dancer when he was younger.

He said, "Here you are, my dears."

He chain smoked, and looked positively cherubic when he smiled.

We smiled, too. He was a great host, but my parents would hate him.

When I was a little girl, pre-school, I'd heard of dreams, but had never had one. I thought something was wrong so, each morning, I'd tell my mother, "I had a red dream" or "I had a blue dream," and she'd laugh. But my dreams were real, horrible, by the time I met Sam. A car I couldn't stop would speed toward me or green monsters would rip my throat out, so I would stay awake until I was exhausted, falling asleep wherever I happened to be, often in a classroom.

I was panicked: furious that Clark was coming home, furious I was married to him, in a rage over problems that seemed insurmountable. I would have existed on vanilla wafers if Sam hadn't taken me out for dinner each evening.

Sam spent the night with me the night before Clark was due to arrive. But we were at my apartment, rather than his house. Clark phoned about 2 a.m., and I remember Sam went to the bathroom while I talked to Clark. Sam looked sad and sleepy, and I remember saying, "Remember softly," as he went down the stairs a few hours later for what we imagined would be the last time.

When Clark came into my apartment, he put a necklace he'd gotten for me in Turkey around my neck, then asked me to say something I hadn't said in any letters for months, but I couldn't say, "I love you." I said, "I'm hungry, haven't eaten for awhile, and I'm almost out of cigarettes. Let's take a walk."

I ate a hamburger while I listened to him babble about the difficulty of a remote tour and how lonely he'd been and how glad he was to be back with me, his wife, and I remember I felt sick

When we returned to my apartment, Clark said he knew things were bad between us, but he didn't think they were bad enough for us to call it quits. About a month before, I'd been determined to commit suicide one night, but not determined enough to do it.

The landlord of my apartment building received a frantic phone call from one of my friends, who was alarmed when I didn't answer my phone after I had left a class in a weeping rage. I got through the night via a nonstop monologue with my landlord.

I'd even written a suicide note, but when I didn't use it for its intended purpose, I mailed it to Clark. When he didn't mention it, I wanted to ask where he got the idea that something was wrong, but I didn't.

Fifteen hours later, one hour for each month Clark had been gone, he left my apartment. I called his home and when his younger sister answered, I said, "This is Kathleen. Clark's coming home. Be kind to him, his marriage just broke," then I hung up.

Kathleen had been afraid of the dark since the car hit her, but her fear was justified. She could easily stumble and fall. But her fear of open closet doors was irrational. She seemed to believe something would come out of the closet, attacking her. She inevitably shut the closet door before going to bed.

Sam brought me a bag of Tootsie Pops this afternoon. There were two orange, two chocolate, and the rest were cherry (grape and cherry are my favorite) so I was thrilled. I've never liked lemon.

Sam believes there aren't any cravings due to pregnancy. If the woman likes wine (or candy) she can have all she wants and still feel righteous.

I immediately ate a Tootsie Pop, and it was definitely sweeter (more candy tasting?) than other Tootsie Pops I've eaten.

Sam kissed me and said, "You have cherry tasting lips."

"What's wrong with feeling righteous?"

Sam didn't know what he was looking for, but he'd recognize it when he saw it. He'd always trusted his instincts. When he'd been shooting *Borderland*, he knew something was missing near the end. The script cut from a scene in a whorehouse to a confrontation with a Mexican general, and Sam told his assistant director, "I want a walk thing," and it had become one of the pivotal moments in the film. Now he watched the road unraveling before him. He drove on, looking.

They stopped at the Little Alien Inn in Rachel because Sam had heard about the place for years. Probably fifty people lived there, but thousands made pilgrimages to the town, if you could call it that, searching the sky for flying saucers. A group of Japanese men wearing suits stood next to a huge telescope across the Extraterrestrial Highway from the inn, wiping their faces with white handkerchiefs, and some dirty looking kids who were naked screamed in a wading pool between two trailers. You could hear the aluminum siding crack and buckle in the heat. It was over a hundred degrees, and one of the most dismal places he'd ever seen.

.It was almost dark when they reached Tonopah. You could see the heat rising from the highway, and the few trees looked like scorched tin cutouts against the setting sun.

They saw a man in a black cassock, eating dandelions on his hands and knees, and Sam wondered if he was a priest gone mad. A woman beat at some faded red sheets at the edge of town, and Sam imagined she must have purchased them from a brothel. They stopped at an old motel with an aluminum umbrella striped in yellow and rust alongside a pool with no water in it, because it had been a long day, driving, driving, except for the stop in Rachel. The heat was relentless.

The lobby had a decayed rattan sofa next to the registration desk, and the clerk was a blonde with a bad bleach job in her mid-40s. Her roots were showing. She wore a large white hat, tilted to one side, with a wide brim and an ostrich feather, and might have been a retired stripper. Her skin was as white and thin as papier-mache. A yellow light bulb glowed dimly. It was heaven's waiting room gone wrong. When Sam asked where they could get a good meal, she pointed wearily across the street.

An arthritic cowboy wearing Levi's and a blue shirt with pearl buttons sat at the counter, cracking his knuckles. He had huge liver blotches on the backs of his hands and stared at them, as if they belonged to someone else.

An overweight cook wearing a dirty apron spit on the grill to see if it was hot. He had a few whisks of white hair, and you could cast him as what he was, a fry cook in a short order house. When he broke an egg he said, "Oops, I stuck my finger in the yolk of that one," then he held up the finger in question, licking it as if he were testing the wind.

"I think he's drunk," Kathleen said.

They were all drinking too much in Texas. Sam's hands shook so badly in the morning he'd have his driver stop at a bar so Sam could drink a couple of vodka and tonics, something light, to stop the shakes. When he got back into the limo, he'd hold up his hands and tell Chalo, "See? I'm steady. Now we can go."

He'd try to make it until five without drinking, but he usually had a drink in his hand by two. He'd tell Chalo, "Bring me a drink," and Chalo would say, "But, Sam, it's not five o'clock," and Sam would slouch in his canvas director's chair, his cowboy hat pulled down across his forehead, and say, "What time is it in New York?" and Chalo would say, "Five-thirty," and Sam would say, "Then bring me a goddamned drink."

But Sam didn't have to depend on Chalo. His prop man had a tray loaded with a bucket of ice, bottles of vodka, Campari, scotch and soda. The tray had a cord attached to both sides, so Bobby could wear it around his neck, like a peanut vendor at a football game.

Sam would say, "I'll have some soda, some Campari and a splash of vodka," and Bobby would fix Sam's drink and make one for himself. Between takes, they'd think up new schemes for embezzling thousands from the production company. The schemes became more and more elaborate as they drank, more absurd, but it was one way to pass the time, and they both loved the idea of beating the suits out of money.

Even McQueen was drunk a lot of the time. He said, "I don't want to grow old in this business and die with a martini in my hand," but he always had one. He was also trying to cut down on his smoking, but that didn't work very well, either.

They were all destroying themselves but, somehow, the film got made.

Twin Lakes had been formed by glaciers in the mountains above Bridgeport. The lakes were separated by a waterfall and a small creek, and people came there to boat or fish or swim. A biker they'd met in Tonopah had told them about the place.

The village next to the lakes and the surrounding land had been owned by the same family for five generations, something almost unheard of in the modern world, where almost everything—land, money, love—dwindled away. Sam knew the story well. The house he'd been raised in didn't exist any longer.

They had lunch at a small café in the village. Their waitress had a gap between her front teeth and told them, proudly, she was 81. A name tag identified her as Bonnie, and Sam wondered if her last name was Blue. She couldn't weigh more than ninety pounds and was five feet tall. The youngest waitress was probably in her 50s.

Sam said, "The people who own the place obviously aren't guilty of age discrimination."

"They tried hiring some younger women, but they were always phoning in sick or something. Their car broke down, their kid had a runny nose, they had a fight with their boyfriend. Me, I'm here, no matter what. I'm dependable." Bonnie shrugged and poured ice water into their plastic glasses.

Sam thought about ordering a Mono Burger, which consisted of a beef patty, a hot dog and cheese, but it seemed too weird so he ordered a Club Style Croissant.

After lunch, he and Kathleen walked beneath the huge pines that surrounded the lake. There was no breeze, so the pine needles were still as stone. A young woman wearing a bright red bikini was water skiing, and several people who were obviously senior citizens were walking their dogs along the shore, lulling the afternoon away. Sam wondered if he was obviously a senior, wondered if people thought he was Kathleen's father, but it didn't matter. Much.

Matterhorn Peak, 12,281 feet high, according to Bonnie, loomed above them. There was still snow on the mountain, although it was June now. Bonnie had also told them the terrain was similar to that of the Swiss Alps, but Sam had never been to Switzerland.

They walked along, holding hands in the filtered green light that came through the trees.

The phone had rung for at least a week after Kathleen had moved in with Sam. It seemed as if everyone she'd ever met had tried to convince her she should stay with Clark, giving her marriage a chance. Even the priest who'd married them was supposed to call, someone said, but he must have had more sense than the others. Sam wondered why she'd put up with all their ranting, but she was probably numb that first week.

One of her mother's friends had phoned at seven in the morning and said, "I hope I'm not interrupting something," hoping she had.

It was amazing how smutty so-called good people could be. A lot of them seemed to think Sam and Kathleen never got out of bed. That you just fucked all the time when you lived in sin. Sam was surprised people still said things like that.

Even Clark had called, insisting Kathleen was drugged. Sam had begun to laugh when she said, "I'm not on anything," because the whole thing was so absurd. The best the poor fool could do when it came to imagining how she could leave him was to conclude she was on drugs. Kathleen thought Clark must have heard Sam laughing because his voice suddenly got very tight and he said, "Goddamn you," and hung up.

My mother claimed she didn't understand why I left Clark. He was religious, he loved his mother, he couldn't have done anything wrong, he was just trying to get me back when he broke into my apartment and took all my clothes and jewelry and personal belongings. He wore a white hat. She crooned.

I received an ungrammatical, misspelled and badly typed letter from Clark shortly after I received the formal divorce papers. I guess his attorney advised him to send it on the off-chance I might have the serial numbers on some of the items Clark stole. He told me to pick up any of my personal belongings or he'd dispose of them, then he added, "The space could be better used for my personal belongings."

What personal belongings? Thirty cheap paperbacks and two wooden ship models.

I answered the letter, listing five items I wanted. Two of them were jewelry boxes from my father, one was a velvet skirt my aunt made for me just before she died, one was a particular cook book, and the final item was a blender. I told him to send me the five things C.O.D., but I never got anything back.

Sam and I went to the mall and looked at some cribs and baby stuff. There was a nice saleslady who told us exactly what we would and wouldn't need and didn't pressure us to buy anything. I always thought people buy way too much for their baby, and Sam never thought about it. He left everything to Edie and Karen.

When the lady said some children won't stay in their cribs, Sam was amazed to learn I slept in one till I was seven. He says he can't remember sleeping in one. I was a tiny child, I'm barely over five feet now, and I was always the littlest in my grade.

I can't remember being disturbed by sleeping in a crib. I imagine I liked the security of the wooden bars, although, much later, I absolutely loathed the steel side bars, similar to those on a crib, for all those months I was in the hospital. Toward the end of my stay in one hospital—I was much stronger by that time—when the night nurse wouldn't leave the side rail down, I'd pick it off and drop it—Clatter! Bang! Bang!—on the floor.

They sat at the round redwood table in their backyard in Sacramento. The moon was low on the horizon, diffused by exhaust fumes and the dust that blew across the city from the rice paddies, the trees wrinkled with wind. Searchlights swept the sky, probably heralding the premiere of a new hamburger stand. Sam tried not to be too cynical these days, but it didn't always work.

"You have to promise not to make fun of me if I tell you… something," Kathleen said.

"I never make fun of you." Her face was incandescent. It glowed. "Well, almost never."

She spoke slowly. "For about a week now, I've had the feeling… you're going to die."

"I'm trying to fall apart with as much style as possible, but I'm not ready to die—yet." He smiled.

"Be serious," Kathleen said.

"I am serious."

"I know it's irrational, but—"

"What do you think I'll die from?"

"I don't know. A heart attack. Maybe you'll be hit by a car."

Sam remembered someone he'd dated saying, "We arrange things, then they fall apart. We arrange them again, then we fall apart," and it had been true then. Maybe Kathleen thought things were falling apart, that the center couldn't hold, but that was difficult to imagine. Maybe it was the feeling that nothing lasts, at least nothing good, but that didn't seem likely, either. She could be superstitious at times, but she was upbeat. Her first word coming out of her nine week coma had been "yes" for a reason.

"What do you think we should do?" he asked.

"Probably nothing. Just hope it goes away." She paused. "I'll tell you one more thing."

"What's that?"

"I won't tell my mother if you die," she said.

His driver in Texas had told him, "When you are nobody and have nothing, you depend on your troubles for self-respect," but they all had their troubles and they had nothing to do with one's self-respect or lack of it.

McQueen had a sore throat the entire time they were shooting, but he had always been a hypochondriac. He had the production nurse examine him, but she just gave Steve some aspirin and hot tea so he called his doctor in Beverly Hills and was told he should consult a specialist in Austin.

The doctor there said Steve had a nodule on his vocal cords, common among people who used their voices a lot, and that he should have it removed eventually, but there was no hurry. Steve wasn't reassured. He asked the doctor, "Give it to me straight," as if he were reciting a bad line in a movie. "Do I have the Big C?"

'No, you do not," the doctor said.

That would come later.

In a few months they'd awaken in the middle of the night and one of them would have to go into the next room to feed the baby. Or to change its diapers. In a few months they wouldn't be able to sleep-in during the mornings because the baby would probably be crying. In a few months they wouldn't be able to make love on a whim, as they had earlier in the day, when they got out of the shower. First, one of them would have to check the baby. But it wasn't the end of a life style, only the modification of one. What existed would take on new meaning and depth. Hanging around with Kathleen had made Sam an optimist.

Now they often had the feeling that they were being watched by a hidden stranger they'd created. The one who walks within, as a friend put it. Often, now, they'd discuss the baby or the things they'd need for its arrival, rather than whispering—why did they always whisper?—little erotic things.

Now, instead of saying, "Let's make love," Sam would say, "Do you think we should paint the baby's room?"

I got my second issue of American Baby *magazine yesterday. I'm supposed to get the first six issues free, then I guess I'm supposed to subscribe. This issue was devoted to nutrition, and I read it in bed.*

Magazines devoted to the care of infants depress me, books I've read on caring for babies depressed me, because they all deal with "must do right" things. The mother "must" have live-in help, preferably a trained baby nurse, for a couple of weeks after the birth. Having the baby "must" be an expensive procedure. Caring for the baby at home "must" be a detailed, full-time job. Feeding the baby "must" be done according to measurement. Like reading a sex manual, all the joy is antiseptically removed.

Even my mother asked if I were going to hire a practical nurse to help out after the baby is born.

Neither Sam nor I ever knew anyone personally who hired a baby nurse, and he knew a lot of people with money.

My mother's logic is that she didn't have the problems I do, problems resulting from the residual effects from the accident. My logic is that I've compensated for any difficulties. I automatically turn my head, rather than moving only my eyes to the left in order to avoid seeing double. I automatically use my left hand rather than my right for any task requir-ing dexterity, such as applying make-up. I automatically bend from the waist rather than the knees. I automatically am cautious when I walk; all the walls in our house have my fingerprints on them. The average person, unless very perceptive, wouldn't be aware of any difficulties I have, because my movements are natural now.

But grace isn't my middle name.

They lay next to one another after they'd made love in the pale vi-olet light of dawn, the sky outside their window a blur. The silhouette of her body was like a range of distant hills, soft, mysterious, alluring. He'd imagined he could never love anyone again when Sara had died, but he'd been wrong.

Sam said, "I'm not dead yet."

"No, you certainly aren't," Kathleen said.

She stood, naked, before the full-length mirror across the room from the bed in the light that was now lilac. She held a pale yellow sundress made of gossamer before her, so Sam could see her breasts through the fabric. They were beginning to swell slightly, almost im-perceptibly. Sam thought she examined her image to see how she'd changed, but he'd spent most of his life looking at things through a lens. Maybe she was just trying to decide how the dress would look on her, what to wear, as she went out into a new day.

He'd never been introspective, possibly because he'd been afraid to discover what he'd learn, but, more and more, these days, he looked inward, and found small joys within himself that had been hidden. But, even at his worst, he'd been a sentimental fool. He'd just tried to hide that part of himself until he'd met Sara, and now… Now he came to Kathleen bearing roses and laughter in the champagne col-ored light of late afternoon. It was more than enough. Even making films didn't seem very important now. He had a life, but he and Kathleen still needed to get out of Sacramento. There had to be a better place to live.

Yesterday, I went to see my o.b. Everything is progressing well, but I need to make a drastic cut in my salt intake. (I love salt! It improves the taste of everything except soup.) I'm gaining too much weight and the salt retains the fluids. The doctor gave me a list of foods high in salt and calories. No cookies, no cake, no pie, no candy, no crackers, no potato chips, no canned soups, no canned vegetables (that's easy, I hate canned vegetables), no table salt. I was so disgusted when I got home that I threw out my malted milk balls. But I kept my Tootsie Pops.

My mother phoned this morning. She wondered what my o.b. had to say. I told her he confirmed her guess that I'd have a girl. I have no idea how she'd come to that conclusion, but I don't know how she decides anything. When I said I had to cut back on my salt intake because of my weight, she asked how much I weigh, then said, "My God, you've never been that heavy."

Last night I took a darvon for the pain in my legs, then I lay next to Sam, feeling the pain go. I thought I'd be able to stay awake for awhile, but any drug, in addition to what it's supposed to do, knocks me out. I sensed he wanted to make love, which would ordinarily be enough, but I fell asleep.

When Sam awakened me at 11:30, I got up, brushed my teeth and came back to bed. I'd slept off the initial pain and drowsiness, so I said, wide-eyed, "I feel better now."

The cuckoo clock Sam hated cuckooed twelve times as he climaxed.

Clouds in the high country perched above ridges where the highways disappeared, so it was easy to imagine you were driving into heaven. But they were only driving into Virginia City, which some people thought was close enough to heaven. Others thought it was closer to the other place, but it was all a matter of perspective.

The board sidewalks, the overhanging wooden canopies, some of the old mansions and the opera house survived, and some of the saloons still had swinging doors. The frontier spirit lived on, especially on the Fourth of July.

Bagpipers were playing "Yankee Doodle Dandy" as they came parading down the street. There were cowboys and cowgirls, politicians and prostitutes, the staid, the young, the old. You could hear gunshots and honky-tonk pianos, banjos, guitars, and someone was playing "Johnny Comes Marching Home" on a trumpet, even though that was a Confederate song and Nevada had gone Union.

There were horses, Corvettes, Model T's, llamas, dogs, mules and flags--flags everywhere--a dizzying blur of red, white and blue. The heat crackled. Fireworks exploded. The beer flowed.

A lady dressed as Julia Bullete, a famed courtesan, went by. Julia had lived in the dim glow of red lights behind drawn shades. Sam had read her funeral was the largest ever held in Virginia City because she'd performed so many charitable acts and brought love—or what might pass for it—to men who had none.

When the parade ended, Sam and Kathleen went into the Bucket of Blood. It was probably the most famous saloon in a town famous for its saloons. Someone was playing "The Streets of Laredo" on a guitar on a small bandstand in one corner. He had droopy eyes and a walrus mustache and was probably sixty. A huge diamond ring on his left hand glittered as he played.

A man wearing a beret asked a woman on the stool next to him, "What kind of a world is it when poets carry credit cards?"

She had a face like an unmade bed and dressed like an aging prostitute, all rhinestones and wrinkles.

"Why ask me?" she said. "I hated poetry in high school and never got over it."

That was one of the tragedies of American life, Sam thought. Some people never got over things. He ordered half a carafe of chardonnay, sitting at a scarred round wooden table with Kathleen, listening to the guitar player.

The east side of the Sierras reminded Sam of the California he'd grown up in. He and Kathleen saw a sign saying RADIATOR WATER, and he remembered his parents carrying burlap bags filled with water that hung from the bumper of their car in case the radiator boiled over. Another sign said IN THE NAME OF JESUS GUARANTEED USED TIRES. It was next to a Confederate flag and half a dozen tow trucks. The people in rural California and Nevada took their religion seriously. They had a Bible in one hand and a Coors in the other and, sometimes, a six-gun strapped to their hip. It brought back a simpler time.

Sam liked the huge pinto skies and the way the light spread itself across the mountain ranges and the forlorn country bars where the failed gods drank.

An old woman they saw in a bar in Big Pine leaned toward a middle aged man who sat across from her and said, "Your father was always half crazy, and the other half was on medication. The only real thing he shared with anybody was a bottle and broken dreams." The windows in the bar were cracked, held together with silver duct tape, and peanut shells covered the floor. The old woman's eyes wore the pink and bruise of grief, and the man who must have been her son nodded mutely.

Crossing into Nevada, they saw four doe leap across the road in front of them, as if they were swimming in air--they were that graceful--then they disappeared into the sagebrush, and Sam realized he'd, finally, found a place to live, to settle with Kathleen, even though he hadn't found the setting for a sequel to *The Heist.*

A thin friend says, "A heavy person pays a heavy price in our culture." I laughingly agree with his wit, while ten pounds hides, quivering, under my smock. Handfuls of vanilla wafers settle among my ribs. I worry while making love that my thighs are too much of an obstacle. I buy grapefruit diet capsules at the store and make an enemy when the lady says, "You don't have to worry." I tell her, "Bullshit, too."

Sam and I looked at some more cribs last night. My mother says the crib has to have a stabilizer bar to prevent accidental collapse. None of the ones we saw had one, but I noticed the cribs were screwed together so they couldn't collapse, unless the baby had a screwdriver.

I bought a pair of pajamas. The legs on them need to be hemmed, but I expect that because all the pants I buy are too long. I learned to do a hem stitch when I was nine.

I also bought my first maternity clothes, "fat clothes." I got a pair of blue jeans with a stretch panel in front and a long sleeved top. Most maternity clothes have bright flowery colors and are generally garish and ill fitting. I hate puffy sleeves and lace.

No wonder pregnant women look like fat angels.

There was a rainbow overhead as they crossed the state line into Nevada. Kathleen said, "It's a good omen," as Sam drove into the yellow and green light of a late-August afternoon. He'd never believed in omens but, this time, he thought she might be right.

When they reached Fernley, they turned south on Highway 95A, heading toward Yerington. They'd bought a home there, after selling the one in Sacramento. It was an impulse, but it seemed right. Most things did, these days.

The Nevada skies were clean and fiercely blue and at night the bright hard stars shimmered like white stones in a creek, and you could smell the leaves burning in small towns in the fall. The trees alongside the road stood in chandelier brilliance and silks of clouds skittered across the sky and the sun seemed to change its shape, becoming an arrowhead, an hour glass, a top, and the sweet wind that came up late each afternoon plucked at the treetops. A windmill flashed its blades in the distance, the light bouncing off of them like semaphores. The distant hills were a pale purple and blue, shimmering until they seemed electric in the late afternoon.

Sam had never felt so in touch with a place.

Welcome home, welcome home.

The trees still dripped water and there were shining drops in the center of some flowers Sam didn't know the names of, but he could learn. You could always learn.

They saw men baling hay and alfalfa, getting ready for winter, alongside the road. Behind them, cattle grazed in the fields. A shining white horse rubbed its neck on a fence, and they could hear quail calling since they had the top down and drove slowly. Fall came early to the high country.

"Yes is now," Kathleen said.

Sam had awakened around three the first night they were there. He'd gone outside, standing on the porch, breathing. The moon was the color of milk and the mountains seemed edged with phosphorus, and he marveled that he was still alive.

There had been too many women whose names Sam couldn't remember, too many cigarettes, too many drinks and the bleary mornings after when they'd been shooting the film in Texas. The women had come and gone like a line in a poem Sam didn't remember the name of, although he remembered reading it in college.

McQueen had inflamed hemorrhoids, aggravated by years of pounding on a motorcycle seat, and wore two sanitary napkins to ease the pain and cut down on the bleeding. He said he understood what women went through, although he knew even less about women than Sam did in those days. Steve could be petty and mean and even brutal when he thought he was losing control, and he was almost always out of control in Texas.

In a scene where he was supposed to slap Ali, he hit her so hard she began to cry. He was also afraid of the dark.

He told Sam, "I have more and more doubts about acting. Sure, sometimes I get that buzz going and know I'm doing good work, but the kick just isn't there most of the time," which was something he'd never tell a woman.

A lot of the scenes called for Ali to drive a car and to use a handgun, but she didn't know how to drive when the film had begun and she'd never fired a gun. By the time the film ended, she drove adequately and she was an expert with a pistol. She said, "I'd never thought of myself as a violent person but, with the guns, I really got into it. Doing those scenes was like being in the middle of the war." She was the only person involved with *The Heist* who learned anything, but she still married Steve.

He stood in the kitchen once he'd come back into the house. The walls were pale blue, like a pair of faded Levi's, and there was a door leading to the two car garage. The floor was a reddish brown tile. Terra cotta. He drank a glass of water, trying to get the feel of the place, then he went back into the bedroom.

Kathleen was awake when he got back into bed.

"Did I leave the milk out?"

She drank more milk, less alcohol, as her pregnancy progressed. The baby was still months away, but its presence became more tangible each day.

"I didn't notice… I don't think so."

He watched her sit on the edge of the bed in the soft glow of the nightlight, putting her blue slippers on, because she was almost phobic about walking barefoot, then he listened to her soft steps as she went down the hall.

He was almost asleep when she returned.

She said, "The milk was in the refrigerator."

He stretched his left arm out, lying on his back, so she could rest her head against it when she got back into bed. He knew she'd ask or tug at him if he didn't.

"I feel big," Kathleen said. "BIG."

"This is just the beginning," Sam said.

He listened to the garbage truck coming down the street just before dawn. He remembered a line from a Lawrence Ferlinghetti poem, about the garbage men parading, although they were just doing their job in the early morning hours.

Sam watched the light gradually brighten as the sun came through the wooden shutters, heralding another day, and Kathleen slept.

I met my new o.b. today, Dr. Casey, in Carson City. Sam and I did some shopping while we were there. I got another maternity outfit, cream colored slacks and a smock top to match. One of the tops was so garish, I'd have looked like a pregnant Easter egg. And another was so full of fruits and leaves, I'm sure a bird would have pooped on me as it flew over while I was wearing it. Unbelievable how difficult it is to find decent looking "fat clothes."

I also shopped for a bra. For a couple of weeks now I've been aware of a heavy, swollen feeling in my breasts. I flunk the Ann Landers' bra test, where you put a pencil under your breasts to see if they'll support it.

I told Dr. Casey I hadn't worn a bra since I was 19 and he said, "I wouldn't worry about it, so long as you aren't uncomfortable." Well, I was, so I bought three of them: one yellow, one pale orange, and one white. Possibly, after I'm done with this baby business, I can go back to being braless, but Sam says he'll love me no matter what.

They were barely inside the bar when someone named Merle asked Sam, "How many times have you been married?" and the two old guys sitting next to Merle laughed when Sam said, "Four." He wondered if this was how people in small towns spent their time. Genoa had been the first settlement in Nevada, but only a couple of hundred people lived there.

"You win," Merle said. "Let me buy you a drink."

The barmaid brought him a beer, but Kathleen had coffee. It was served in a huge cup with a picture of the bar on it, along with the words Nevada's Oldest Thirst Parlor.

Merle was probably Sam's age. He talked fondly about growing up in Richmond, California in the 40s and early 50s. It was a time, he said, when everyone wore suits and ties, and he claimed there were seven movie "palaces" in Richmond when he was a teenager, but Sam only remembered the smog and smoke from the oil refineries there.

Merle said the California he'd grown up in was gone, not just Richmond, but Los Angeles and San Francisco, and he'd moved to Nevada three years ago. He said, "California changed, and I didn't know how to change with it, so I left."

"Me, too," Sam said.

They shared half a carafe of chardonnay after they'd had dinner at Casino West. It was six-tenths of a mile from their home, so they'd walked. The barmaid had long black hair held back with a pony tail and she had the clearest complexion Sam had ever seen. She could have been a Cover Girl. She'd moved to Yerington from Apple Valley, escaping from California, and she sang snatches from hit songs as she worked.

They walked back home under a vast starry sky that twinked and glittered. It was dizzying. They were holding hands and trying to watch where they were going, looking up, up, as the stars made their slow circumference across the dark, and they were giddy. Sam almost felt young again.

We ate our first meal at home yesterday. I broiled hamburgers, but the grease in the broiling pan, which was lined with tin foil, caught on fire. It was scary, even though it was just a little baby fire. Sam promptly put it out by smothering it. If I'd been alone, I'd have used salt.

I don't think Sam had ever turned a stove on, but he wanted to show me "the perfect way" to make French fries. He heated the canola oil until it was boiling, then dropped a handful of frozen fries into the skillet.

The hamburgers and fries tasted fine, but grease splattered everywhere, so we spent part of the afternoon cleaning the stove top, the wall and the side of the refrigerator.

"Maybe eating at home isn't such a hot idea," Sam said.

I'm eating my last Tootsie Pop (cherry, of course) from the bag Sam brought me when we were still in Sacramento. I cheated for breakfast and ate a glazed donut. I hate dieting, but I hate exercising even more.

I was always the last one chosen for any team sport when I took gym in high school. That was one blessing from the accident. I never had to take gym again. I was permanently excused from it all through college. Of course physical therapy is nothing more than a series of exercises, but they were professionally administered and I was able to see the results day by day when I came out of my coma. I was determined to get on and off the toilet by myself. It took five months, because everything was broken.

It was the greatest achievement of my life.

They eased into the day, staying in bed until ten, although they'd been awake for hours. It was all new to Sam. Being domestic. It had been a strange dawn, the overcast sky diffusing a tea-colored light over their bed. He remembered a time when every sunrise came to him like a testimony to personal failure, although he'd been famous, at least in Hollywood.

Last night they'd bathed in water that was blue from some bath beads Kathleen bought, and Sam realized he'd never bathed in blue water. There had been a time, several times, when he imagined he'd done everything, that there was nothing new left for him, but he'd been wrong.

After they'd bathed, they sat in the large sunroom that had been added on to the house. They watched the honey-colored moon through the huge windows, wrapped in large fluffy white robes, sitting on a loveseat across from Sam's desk. The wind stirred the leaves in the apple and cherry trees in the backyard.

"I never wanted another relationship with anyone once I knew my marriage had failed," Kathleen said, "and now… here we are."

"Here we are," Sam repeated. "I wonder why it lasted as long as it did."

"My mother told me marriage was for life."

"I believe that."

"Married four times?"

"Yes. Married four times." He watched the moon, low on the horizon, and said, "I want you to know I don't want anyone else." He knew she worried about her "poor, swollen, lumpy body," although she exaggerated. He held her to him in the moon shadow. "I'm glad you're my wife."

"Me, too," she said.

They packed salami and roast beef sandwiches, a small bag of potato chips, a bottle of Mumm's champagne and two crystal glasses wrapped in a towel to prevent breakage before leaving home. The top on the Cadillac was down.

As Sam backed out of the driveway, the leaves on the locust tree lifted like green feathers in the wind. Across the street, the tips of the leaves on the catalpa tree were tinted with sunlight.

They drove past cottonwoods and fields filled with corn and onions, and watched some speckled horses run through a pasture, past a barn with a corrugated roof that was the color of an old nickel. There was a sign alongside the road on the right: *Bulls For Sale. Pioneer Territory*, another sign said.

Kathleen sang, "On a picnic we will go, for it's summer time you know," then faltered and said, "and I love to—I forget the word---in the park." She laughed when Sam said, "Fuck," her hair streaming behind her, "No, not *that*. My word had two syllables."

They drove through Wilson Canyon, then Sam parked beside some picnic benches alongside the Walker River, 17 miles from the house. The light on the water was phosphorescent, and the hills in the distance were a faded yellow.

They walked along the river's edge, then sat at a wooden picnic table. Kathleen unwrapped their sandwiches while Sam opened the champagne, filling their glasses. They toasted each other and the baby to be, the crystal chiming, and the tops of the pines crackled in the wind.

Some friends hosted a going away party for them the week before they left Sacramento. A lawyer who worked for the Franchise Tax Board and who saw five hundred movies a year had been there, along with the owner of a small bookstore and a woman poet. The lawyer was gay and Jewish and he had impeccable taste, at least it seemed that way to Sam, since Marvin had seen all of his movies. The bookstore owner was bald, in his late thirties and was one of the kindest people Sam had ever known. Richard gave a short speech, saying how much he'd miss Sam and Kathleen, just before dinner was served, and he cried. The poet was in her late sixties and read a poem she'd written for them that ended, "Anywhere the two of you live will be fine, even the long miles from the valley. Think of us as insurance against goodbye." The one person who didn't come worked part-time for the State of California and had told Sam and Kathleen they were "committing suicide" moving to a rural town in Nevada where they didn't know anyone, but Jacob had always been strange. Marvin said, "Jacob's paranoid-schizophrenic, and those are his good qualities." No one at the party missed him.

They awakened simultaneously. Kathleen removed the pillow she kept between her legs each evening to minimize the pain.

She said, "Clark always complained when I slept with a pillow like that."

Sam didn't say anything, because he didn't want to have a conversation about Clark, didn't want to complain. About anything.

Sometimes she called Sam The Greatest Kisser in the Northern Hemisphere, and she turned to him now, kissing him, in the persimmon colored light that signaled the beginning of day.

She smiled. "I just want to make sure I'm not with a stranger."

"No more strangers."

"Only you," she said.

"Ditto."

That had been a joke between them at the beginning. Kathleen would compliment him, then he'd say something equally nice to her, and she'd say, "Never return a compliment with a compliment," although she never said why you shouldn't. Maybe it was a rule in some obscure book he'd never read.

They eased into making love gradually, not saying anything, just letting it happen, the way you would let the day happen or the earth rotate, then, later, she lay on top of him, and he could feel her heart beating and, once, he thought he felt the baby moving, but that might just have been something he hoped for, that fruition.

"You know what I like best about you?" Kathleen asked, finally.

"No."

"Everything," she said.

They'd grown so used to the sounds of the slot machines that they no longer heard them when they went into the casino. It was like listening to elevator music. You were never really aware of it.

Sam ordered a dry martini and Kathleen ordered a small glass of chardonnay, and there were bowls filled with pretzels on the bar before them.

He pushed the bowl to Kathleen. "Have a pretzel."

"No thanks," she said.

I remember people getting mouth and throat burns from eating lye-coated pretzels when I was in college. Seventy people were hospitalized in

Solano and Sacramento Counties. I was worried when the news broke, because I had an opened box of pretzels in the cupboard. But mine were made by Nabisco, not Pepperidge Farms.

I hadn't realized it was a common practice to put lye on the pretzels to give them a glaze. Usually, the lye crystals dissolved into a form of salt, but something in the process had gone wrong, and nineteen thousand cases of pretzels had been recalled.

I told people it would be years before I ate another pretzel, and some of my friends said they'd never eat one again, but we all did.

It was distressing. There were rat hairs in hot dogs, lye on pretzels, and loads of artificial stuff pumped into everything. It was amazing what the human body could endure, but I knew that better than anyone.

Kathleen liked to tell people the best veggie burger she ever ate had bacon on it, because it was interesting to see their expressions. A meal without meat wasn't a meal to her. When Sam ordered the T-bone steak with mashed potatoes, she said, "I always thought mashed potatoes were ugly, so I never served them, until one Thanksgiving when I was married to what's his name. I dyed them blue so they were actually pretty, but no one would eat them."

"I wonder why not," Sam said.

Autumn was white wine in the damp grass in the high plains. They'd worried that it might snow in Virginia City, since it was more than six thousand feet high, but the weather was perfect. Cold, but perfect. The night sky was as brilliant as the afternoon's, but it was ten degrees colder than Yerington, and the wind blew small ragged things down the street as they passed The Palace Restaurant & Saloon and the Millionaire's Club of the Washoe.

Kathleen had gone to a shop that only sold things relating to Christmas because she loved the holiday, but thought she wouldn't be able to travel by the time Christmas came because the baby was due then. Sam sat outside, waiting, on the Scrooge Bench, remembering their first Christmas.

They'd had a tree in his bedroom, just before Clark had come back from Turkey, even though Sam imagined they'd never see each other again. But she'd come back less than a day later. It had been beyond his understanding at the time, in some ways it still was, but he'd been grateful. He remembered she'd had that gallant look women sometimes take on in moments of grief, but she was past grieving.

They stopped to look in the window of the Mark Twain Book Store, the yellow light spilling out onto the board sidewalk. An old guy with hair as white as meringue and softly smudged blue eyes leaned against the door. He told the woman next to him, "All men are born with an allowance of one boxcar full of booze that they can drink during their lifetime, and when the boxcar is empty their drinkin' days are done. Some space their allowance out over the years and some consume it all early on." The woman wore a soft buckskin dress that was as yellow as cream in the morning sun. The old guy went on, "I drunk my share by the time I was forty, damn it, and I been lost ever since." He might be lost, Sam thought, but he was still drunk.

Someone playing a guitar sang about adultery and horses and drinking when they passed a saloon, but this was Nevada. One range of mountains followed another, gradually fading in the incandescent moonlight, until the ones furthest away seemed like ghost ranges, and Sam remembered a song Vaughn Monroe had made famous about ghost riders in the sky. It seemed plausible, but most things did, in a place where the sky went on forever.

I hate going to the dentist.

My left hand was resting across my stomach when Dr. Ahlborn examined me. As I got more tense and strained, the baby started to kick violently, and my hand jumped in time with the baby's movements. Ahlborn laughed and said he'd never seen anything like it.

When I went into the next room for the routine cleaning, the baby settled down. (The paste the technician used tasted like St. Joseph's baby aspirin, orange and gritty.) I could feel her flutter occasionally, but she wasn't so violent.

I've read about how important it is for a mother to be stable when the child is pre-natal. Today the baby could sense my mounting stress, tense muscles and their forced relaxation, and she reacted to my discomfort in the only way she could: kicking and kicking and kicking.

Pregnancy seems to bring out the worst in people. When I walked into the grocery store, the clerk immediately wanted me to remove my jacket so she could see how big I am. And Julia was pushy about it. She didn't see anything wrong with her request. When I went into the drugstore yesterday, the clerk, Ann, made a big, very vocal fuss about my state.

Should I go around naked to satisfy their curiosity?

As soon as women begin to get a shape, they lose their individuality, except for those who know them personally. They become bodies. Men look at their asses or breasts to see if they measure up to the one at home, and other women look for signs of obesity or aging.

Someone who'd worked on our house saw us downtown and said I looked like I was ready to bloom, then George winked at Sam and said, "That's the way to keep 'em, barefoot and pregnant." I was wearing black wedge shoes.

Most men are at a complete loss when faced with a pregnant woman. Either they ignore her, say something stupid, or smile condescendingly.

A woman's body gets gazed at a lot. If she's pregnant, people seem to feel it's all right to look or touch or ask stupid questions or to make rude remarks.

Sometimes I just want to hide.

A heavyset blonde in her twenties came running out of the Lyon County Courthouse, followed by a woman who might have been her anorexic sister. Sam and Kathleen watched as the huge door banged behind them. The blonde began to cry, and the woman who might be her sister hugged her. The day burned in glory, but not for the blonde. She screamed, "It isn't fair," and cried harder.

"Most things aren't," Sam said.

Sam hired his daughter as a dialogue director when he was shooting *The Heist*. She'd said, "I'm interested in filmmaking and in having a father," but it not only hadn't worked, it had been a disaster. Ellie told him he wasn't fun to be around, but he hadn't hired her to have fun. He'd hired her to do a job, but she'd been too busy hanging around with some long-haired guy. He'd fired her three times in one night, then she went off to Mexico with the boyfriend.

Ellie later told a reporter, "I got tired of him being mean to me. I'm not a good doormat. He'd take your ego, throw it on the ground and stomp on it. Then he'd do it over and over. I got sick of it, so I'd talk back in front of the crew. I'd yell at him."

She claimed he never gave her a reasonable explanation of what he expected her to do, but he thought her title explained everything. She was supposed to help people with their lines.

Sam was hurt she blamed him for her failure, but no one said life had to be fair.

They hadn't noticed the brassiere that hung from the ceiling the first time they'd come to Genoa. Maybe he'd been flummoxed by the guy asking how many times he'd been married.

The barmaid said there had been dozens of bras tacked to the ceiling when Raquel Welch had been making a picture in the area. When someone asked Raquel to contribute her bra, she said she'd do it if all the others were removed, which is what happened, at least according to local legend. It sounded like the story a good public relations man would make up.

Kathleen asked the barmaid if anything "original" still existed, besides the building, and the barmaid said, "You're sitting at it," but the medallions on the ceiling were also original. So was the red oil lamp, which was lit every New Year's Eve.

The Genoa Bar was a place of high old times. Willie Nelson, Merle Haggard, Waylon Jennings and Johnny Cash had all been there. So had every governor of Nevada.

The barmaid said, "You may walk in a stranger, but you'll leave here a friend."

Kathleen thought it was as good a place as any to hide out.

I told Sam I'm going to breast feed our baby. A manufactured formula can't compete with the natural antibodies, the convenience (no bottles to sterilize or to break), the excellent general nutrition or the comfort (for both mother and child). With a breast fed infant there are no digestive problems or bowel movement problems, as there tend to be with bottle fed babies. The final clincher, according to Consumer's Research Magazine, is that breast fed infants suffer dramatically less from infantile obesity than bottle fed newborns because a breast fed baby will stop suckling when she's had enough, whereas a bottle fed infant is often encouraged to finish the bottle. Infantile obesity often leads to childhood and adult obesity.

Sam smiled when I told him all that.

"It sounds like you have it all figured out," he said.

The maple leaves were pumpkin-colored now that fall had come. They passed fields filled with the brown burn of corn, weeds curling around the dead stalks, but there was a stark beauty to it all.

They explored the territory, driving north toward Pyramid Lake. It would make an interesting location for a film, but there wasn't a bank to rob.

The water in the lake was calm, cerulean, but the land around it was desiccated. It was as if the sun had baked the color out of everything. It was a scene from *The Twilight Zone*. Sam could imagine Rod Serling saying, "It is a land of light and shadow."

They stopped at a general store in Empire to buy Cokes. It was the only store for the next 70 miles, according to a sign. There were stacks and stacks of Pabst Blue Ribbon Beer inside the store. Outside, there was a gypsum mine, a few ranches and the brilliant light of the high desert.

Kathleen said, "It's as if someone shot the sun in your face," then they got back into the car and drove north to Gerlach, which reminded Sam of those wind-blown towns you saw in the movies, towns where tourists were forever lost in the desert.

They had lunch at Bruno's Country Club, although it was unlike any country club Sam had seen. Bruno's had a few booths with torn vinyl next to the dirty windows and the linoleum was worn, but the place probably seemed like a palace to the three hundred people who lived there.

A red-headed woman in her late forties sat next to someone with a drooping handlebar mustache that was tobacco stained. He wore a huge black Stetson and looked like he might have been a bit player in B-westerns. Maybe he had.

The red-head told him, "I always seem to meet men at the bottom of their game, men who live at the cold end of the street."

He nodded, his pale blue eyes watering, and said, "Don't grieve on what you can't change."

It seemed like good advice to Sam.

Sam and I spent the night in Reno. We could easily have driven home, but we wanted this to be a weekend outing. Probably our last before the baby comes.

I didn't sleep well, which was no surprise. I seldom do when I'm away from home. Strange bed, strange surroundings. I'm always worried that the door isn't properly locked.

I imagined some robbers got the key to our room from the maid. And I furthered the fantasy. I was going to pretend to go into labor when the robbers appeared. I hoped the robbers—there were two of them—would be so alarmed they'd immediately leave, forgetting about the credit cards and cash, of course. I smiled in the murky motel darkness.

I managed to sleep for a couple of hours after that, because I knew I could deal with the robbers.

They stopped at a used bookstore outside of Reno. There were some horses on the property next door, and the road was lined with rural route mailboxes on posts. The bookstore was in what used to be a garage, and the owner's wife operated a beauty parlor out of a spare bedroom.

Jim was probably forty-five, a little over six feet tall and stocky, like a wrestler, and he was bald. Kathleen thought he resembled Ken Kesey. He sat behind a large desk, drinking tea. There was a poster of an American flag with the words FUCK COMMUNISM printed across it on the wall behind him.

He said he'd owned a bookstore in Oakland, California ten years ago, but he got tired of being harassed by the police for selling poetry books with dirty words and for some small press magazines, particularly *The Marijuana Review*. It had been edited by a poet in Cleveland who'd finally killed himself due to police harassment, but the cops hated the FUCK COMMUNISM poster, too. Jim finally asked a stammering cop, "Surely, you don't approve of Communism, do you?"

He said he'd sold thousand of other publications, but the cops arrested him for being a narcotics dealer, believing anyone who sold *The Marijuana Review* had to be one. He spent three days in jail, because bail was set at ten thousand dollars and he didn't have the money.

Charges were finally dropped after sixteen months, and there was never a trial. He said the cops tried to plant marijuana in his store, so he'd go into the shop and immediately lock the door in the morning, looking for "plants." He found one, although his reasons for leaving Oakland were more complex than that. They were the same ones you heard from people leaving cities everywhere: traffic, smog, crime in the streets. Sometimes it seemed as if America was falling apart. Maybe it was.

Jim said, "I didn't want to carry a gun to work, so I got out of there."

"Pretend you're watching a ship move across the horizon. Pretend you're watching a tennis match, watching the ball go back and forth as the players volley. Relax."

The women lay on blankets on the concrete floor of a community center south of Carson City. They were contracting and relaxing their vaginal muscles, contracting and relaxing, as they listened to their coach, Charlotte, tell them how to "Kagel."

They were supposed to exercise their muscles two hundred times a day, as they sat in their cars at stoplights, while they were on the toilet, as they talked to their girlfriends on the telephone, even as they stood at the stove, whipping potatoes, their vaginas fluttering, picking up the rhythm of what it was they did. It was as if they were members of a high school band, nervous about their performance, missing a beat or two. People really were uncomfortable with their bodies, uncomfortable with sex, Sam thought. He'd never imagined he'd attend a natural childbirth class, but he wanted to be with Kathleen when the baby came, so the class was a necessity. It was the first of eight they were going to attend.

The husbands were even more nervous than the women. Larry had a white number 19 on his red T-shirt and tried to look past his belly at the floor as if there were something of incredible interest there. Fred, an insurance salesman from Gardnerville, had a button down white shirt with no tie and looked like an Arrow collar ad type who didn't make the cut for the photo shoot. Ernest and his wife, both Washoe Indians, seemed most comfortable. When Charlotte instructed everyone how to do the "Indian Shuffle" exercise, they smiled.

I used to listen to one of the local radio stations when I was a stu-dent at UC-Davis. Sermons were broadcast all day Sunday, in case you'd missed church or couldn't get enough of being preached at, but, other than that, the station was all right. I just tuned out on Sundays.

The station paid tribute to a local housewife each week. She'd win a styling dryer for her home-made hair do. The housewives could be nominated by any member of their family. I could imagine some farmer's wife being nominated and winning. It would probably be the biggest event in her life.

After awhile, the station came up with a new promotion. It paid tribute to the working girl of the week, and I wondered if the "girl" was younger than 18. She got a free wash and set at one of the local beauty parlors.

I asked a classmate, "Did you know working girls are the only ones who can go out to get their hair done? The housewife has to make do with a home Toni?"

The air was as crisp as cellophane in the shimmering light of noon, and huge clouds moved across the sky like waves. The valley had probably been a sea aeons ago.

They passed a gun store with an American flag in front, no surprise. Sam had met someone who worked there, another refugee from California, who referred to Yerington as Redneck Heaven. True enough, but Sam still loved the place. Someone else said the town was one of the last places left in America where Norman Rockwell would feel comfortable, and that was probably true, too. They passed a Rexall Drug Store with ads that had appeared in the *Mason Valley News* ("the only newspaper in the world that gives a damn about Yerington") Scotch-taped to the front windows, and the post office with its community bulletin board listing yard and garage sales.

They crossed the street to Dini's Lucky Club and shared a glass of wine in what was called The Cellar, although the bar was on the same level as the casino. There was a jukebox next to the small stage across the dance floor.

Someone sitting next to Sam stuffed five dollar bills into the poker machine built into the bar, his hands shaking. He told the woman next to him, "I can afford it. I make fifty bucks a day."

Probably, it was just another wasted afternoon in the old couple's lives. Sam imagined their idea of a good day was to watch trash television when they weren't gambling, but he'd wasted more afternoons than he wanted to think about, drinking and whoring, when he wasn't making a movie. He tried not to be too judgmental.

The Cellar was probably no better or worse than a million other bars, but there was something unappealing about the place. It was good to go back outside into the brilliant afternoon light, holding hands, heading home.

He believed in the feeling of beatitude you got when you were rid of rage and in the grace that came from making love, although he'd raged into his fifties, until he'd met Sara. When she was gone, he thought he might rage again, but he was too tired, beyond rage, then he met Kathleen. She'd given him an Italian good luck tooth made of jade shortly after they'd met, but she'd given another made of ivory to her husband, mailing it to him in Turkey. Sam was the one who got lucky. When they came home they stood in the kitchen, hugging. Kathleen said, "You got the prize," not knowing how unequivocally right she was, then they went into the bedroom.

They'd spent three days filming *The Heist* at Huntsville State Penitentiary. McQueen played one of the prisoners, but Sam had cast more than fifty real convicts in the scenes with him. The first scene was shot in the exercise yard the first afternoon they were there.

When the scene wrapped, Sam yelled, "Cut!" and Steve took off toward his dressing room, away from the actual convicts. He was still wearing his prison uniform. The guard dogs had been trained to go after any convict who broke ranks, so they'd come running after him, snarling, ready to tear him to pieces in the sloping afternoon light.

It was over a hundred degrees outside. The heat waves were so intense they were blue, spiraling like an out of control top, and the trees sagged under the sun. A buzzard swept across the circular sky.

Steve's clothes were sweat-stained when he came over to where Sam was standing, a red and blue bandana knotted around his forehead. He leaned against the huge Panavision camera, his eyes shielded by glasses with mirrored lenses. He'd worn them a lot in those days. They'd served two purposes: hiding his bloodshot eyes and whatever emotion he felt.

McQueen raged. "Goddamn it, I barely made it outa that yard alive. Those dogs were ready to tear my ass off, you ignorant son-of-a-bitch."

"Yeah, but it will sure look great on film," Sam said. "You should have seen yourself." In those days, he'd do anything to get the picture made.

Charlotte talked about the "nesting instinct" at our natural childbirth class last night. She said pregnant women often have the urge to wash the walls or to do strenuous house cleaning in preparation for the coming baby. She warned the husbands to beware of the nesting instinct in their bulky wives, because they might overdo things and strain something.

Today, I swept and mopped the kitchen floor, did three loads of laundry, dusted the furniture and vacuumed all the rooms and the hall. I'd shampooed the rug in the front room before the delivery men brought the crib we'd selected. They wore a greasy path through the center of the rug, so I shampooed it again. Charlotte got it right.

I told Sam, "Take me out to dinner. I'm exhausted."

The castle rose up out of Death Valley like a mirage. It was vaguely Moorish or what a Hollywood magnate might have imagined Moorish to be when the castle was under construction. It was part California mission, part Arabian Nights. As someone said, "It is stupendous, colossal, in its own way, an epic." It was also a miracle of sorts, a Technicolor movie created by Cecil B. De Mille, a Mad Hatter's dream.

Kathleen had slept most of the way there, but she often slept when they traveled. The movement of the car lulled her, more so, now that she was pregnant. It beat nesting.

The castle consisted of two concrete buildings that faced each other across an oblong patio. Both structures had red tile roofs and both were topped by wrought-iron weathervanes that showed Death Valley Scotty herding his burros across the sky. It was almost an unimaginable creation, costing more than a million dollars in the 1920s, but no more unimaginable than the man, who claimed to have found gold in the desert.

"It's fucking awesome," they said, simultaneously, then they headed up the path to the castle.

No one but Scotty ever saw the gold mine, so its existence was doubtful. Most people thought Scotty was a huckster who befriended a wealthy, frail man named Albert Johnson, who came from Chicago. No one was sure why Johnson would put up the money for a castle, letting Scotty pretend he'd struck it rich, but Scotty was charismatic, a larger than life character, and maybe he amused Johnson. Maybe it was that simple.

Scotty thought of himself as a monumental creator of fiction. He drank and swore and rolled his own cigarettes, and he liked to wear six-guns and Stetsons. He had blue eyes, white hair and a face burned red by the desert sun. He was short, paunchy, by the time he'd struck it rich, a movie star gone to pot. He liked to lie around the castle when he got older, telling tourists he'd been bitten by a mountain lion. Or a rattler. Or a black widow. Probably he had the gout from too much food and drink, but there was no romance in that, and everything about him had to be romantic—mysterious.

"Whatever he was, or wasn't," Kathleen said, "he certainly dreamed big."

Dr. Casey is so pale he could pass for an albino if he had pink eyes, so slender he might be a stick man brought to life. He wears a pale green smock, similar to something an artist might wear although he is no artist, unless one thinks of him as an artist of the delivery room, a sorcerer of surgery. He wears a dark green bow tie, and his graying hair is crew cut. His brown eyes are enlarged behind his horn rimmed glasses so he seems bemused, although he comes highly recommended.

After he takes my blood pressure and weight, he places his stethoscope against my breast, listening to my heart beat, nodding.

My feet dangle over the edge of the examination table, and I shiver, even though the room is warm. There is something terribly mechanical about the whole process. It is not what I expected when I became pregnant, although I have no idea what my expectations were.

Dr. Casey says, "Your weight is a little higher than it ought to be and your blood pressure is slightly elevated, but we'll be all right there. I'm worried about some swelling in your ankles, though," squeezing my right ankle, as if he thinks I may not know what part of my body he's referring to. "You need to cut down on your salt intake. We don't want to see you ending up in the hospital with toxemia before the baby arrives."

"No, we certainly don't want to see that," I say.

They lay on their left sides, Sam's arms around her, since it was Kathleen's favorite position. Sam cupped her breasts, which had grown fuller each month. When they went out, she wore a bra for the first time since they'd been together, and she complained about being bulky. When she whispered, "I feel unloved," as if it were a secret she wasn't sure she should share, Sam held her so closely he thought they might blend together into one being and, for a moment, he imagined they were one, the starlight filtering through the shutters, bathing their bodies in light. Finally, curled into one another, they slept.

They walked to Casino West when they awakened.

A lone cowpoke sat at the bar, resting his elbows on it, a shot glass and a can of Coors before him. He looked as happy as the dying cowboy in "The Streets of Laredo." He said, "I can't take the weather in Montana no more. You get summer on the Fourth of July, and the rest of the time it's snowin'. I need to get outa there." His face looked like spectralized blue cheese in the light. "I been to three realtors and to every bar in town, but haven't learned nothin', except they're a lot friendlier here than they are at Dini's. I don't expect them to be my buddies because I tip big, but it might be nice if they were civil, maybe pretended to care a little, smiled once in awhile. Here, they knew my name right off."

"We had the same experience," Sam said.

They walked home slowly, star light, star bright. Sam reached out to her each time they came to a curb and had to step down. She was all right when she stepped up.

Kathleen said, "I'm proud of you, Sam."

So many people weren't. "Why?"

"Because you're incapable of being anyone other than who you are."

"You have no idea how much trouble that caused me," he said.

Major Dawson ran fifteen days over its shooting schedule and a million and a half dollars over budget. Someone referred to it as "*Moby Dick* on horseback," but it was conceived as a Civil War epic with a huge cast, then scaled down because the studio heads got scared.

Sam was furious most of the time, firing fifteen people by the time the film wrapped. The gunsmiths didn't bring enough blank ammunition, the guns weren't right, misfiring, and the sound was inferior. Sam yelled at one of the camera men so loudly the guy was never able to operate a camera again. But, as the wardrobe man observed, "Sam didn't need to yell, he could cut you to ribbons with a goddamn whisper and make you lean in to hear it."

In one shot, the star was supposed to lead cavalry troops down a hill toward Sam. When the star asked how he'd done, Sam said, "That was shit! Jesus Christ, you came too slow!"

Chuck said, "You told me to bring them down at a trot."

"The hell I did."

Chuck wheeled his horse around, drew his saber, and charged Sam, missing him by inches. Sam got the shot he wanted, but it hadn't saved the picture. He'd been too obsessed with getting everything right, with not compromising, but it was the only way he'd ever known how to work. A director who was the son of a famous French painter had said, "Evil in Hollywood isn't greed. It's the desire for perfection." Sam had never been impressed with Renoir's work, but he certainly understood evil in Hollywood.

Sam drove through Wilson Canyon, the sunlight dazzling on the Walker River, huge clouds shaped like saucers, big horn sheep hidden in the hills. Everything blurred. I said, "My parents took me to Knott's Berry Farm several times when I was a child. I remember I panned for gold, which was put into a tiny jar for safekeeping, and I remember riding a mule on a trail. My dad took movies of all that. From the movies, I know I was wearing white sandals with white anklet socks. There were a couple of rides. I remember the old fashioned merry-go-round that was pulled by a horse and people sat in swings. I loved that and the jams and jellies they sold. I was fascinated by the glass blowing shop and the piano playing chicken.

"My dad also took movies of me at Disneyland. I still wore traditional white sandals and white anklets, but this time I also wore a hat with feathers.

"At Marine Land of the Pacific, I was wearing a sailor's hat."

Sam wasn't used to hearing me talk so much. I was usually as quiet as the evening. It was as if I'd taken speed, which I hadn't done since I was in college. The words just kept coming.

"What's the point?" Sam asked.

"Maybe there isn't one. It just seemed like a nice story. There aren't enough of them."

We have a short break before our natural childbirth class resumes. Bonnie, the woman on the blanket next to mine, tells me, "I just love to drink beer on the weekends." It is a story she recites each week, so I almost know it by heart now. "I'm not an alcoholic or anything, but when I'm pregnant, which is all I've been for the last couple of years, I'm always afraid I'll hurt the baby. I worry about smoking, too. That movie on TV last night showed how your placenta turns from a healthy red to kind of a sickly looking yellow when you're smoking a cigarette, and all the things you read in these books that Charlotte lets us borrow scare me, but what isn't harmful these days?" It is a question she obviously doesn't expect me to answer.

Bonnie has red hair and freckles and is probably thirty pounds over-weight. Her husband, Larry, is probably a hundred pounds overweight, but he isn't having a baby. He works for the railroad and is gone for days at a time, and Sam says he gets rhapsodic talking about his experiences at the whorehouse. Bonnie won't have sex with him until the baby's born.

Bonnie says, "I normally don't smoke more than ten cigarettes a day. That shouldn't hurt me or the baby too much, should it?" She pauses, but it is another question she doesn't expect me to answer. "My first two babies were healthy, so if something goes wrong this time, I won't blame myself. As soon as this one arrives, I've promised myself a big binge, but the more I think about it, I'd like a series of medium binges. And no more kids. I'm afraid I'll have the figure of a woman who's ninety if I keep this up. But Larry's going to the doctor to see about having a vasectomy while I'm in the hospital. Now, all we have to do is talk about sex and I'm pregnant.

If he doesn't go through with the vasectomy, I'm getting my tubes tied. That's a promise."

The moonlight glinted on the horns of some long horn cattle as they drove south through the Carson Valley. It would make a good scene in a movie, but Sam was probably through making westerns. Maybe he was through with movies, period, but it was something he didn't worry about anymore. They'd cost him more of his sanity than he'd realized at the time.

The studio cut thirty-five minutes out of a picture that had run two hours forty-one minutes, then they cut another ten minutes from it and they did it without Sam's knowledge, let alone his permission. He went to an early screening with one of the actors at the Egyptian Theater in Hollywood, and was absolutely livid when the film ended. The real, bloody, awful things that happened to men in war had been cut out, so the violence seemed exciting, even attractive. It was unforgivable.

Sam's hands were shaking so badly he dropped a pint of whiskey, watching it break on the sidewalk, his body convulsing, as he stood there swaying in the neon light from the marquee. His hands were a ghastly orange, and he thought he was going to throw up.

The actor's wife touched his shoulder, gently. He remembered her fingertips felt warm against his neck. "Sam, easy baby, it's just… it's just a movie. I know, we all feel it should have been a lot better but, Jesus, don't let it destroy you," but it had, momentarily at least.

When Sam drove to the studio a few days later, the guard at the front gate said, "I'm sorry, Mr. Bonner, but I can't let you through."

The name on his parking space had already been painted over, and all the personal belongings from his office were on the floor of the gatehouse in a cardboard box. He'd been fucked-over by another producer.

Another day spent nesting, I wore myself out, and the mop leans against the bathtub like a tired soldier.

We made love last night. That's unusual, night lovemaking, since I've been pregnant. I move more easily in the morning. It had stormed yesterday, and it was still raining when we went to bed. The rain gloom from outside made our room darker than usual. More cozy.

I thought of the W.C. Fields movie Sam and I saw a few months ago. Rod Steiger played the part of W.C. and he was great. The film was built around Fields' relationship with his mistress, and there was a fantastic scene toward the end, when Fields was dying. He'd always said he could sleep most comfortably when it was raining, so his mistress stood outside and sprayed water onto the roof above his bedroom.

It had rained all night. After he'd made the coffee, Kathleen said, "Come back to bed. Hold me," and he did. He knew she liked to make love when it rained, and the light at dawn had been ethereal, coming through the shutters.

They made love for the second time in less than twelve hours. When they'd finished, Kathleen said, "I'll forget what it's like to be on the bottom."

"That doesn't matter," Sam said. "That doesn't matter at all."

Dr. Casey had told them, "The first lesson of yoga is to relax, and the second is to relax even more," so it was almost as if they'd filled a prescription, making love, relaxing, although there was nothing clinical about it. Sam had never felt such solidarity.

They listened to the rain, easing into the new day.

"Sometimes I just lay here and marvel at the wonder off it all," I told Sam. "Here!" I put his hand on top of mine, which was resting on my stomach, then I pulled my hand out from under his. "Now, knead my stomach gently, in an up and down motion." I felt the rippling within. "That moving lump is her foot. Dr. Casey told me the baby has turned."

"You mean she'll be upside down for six weeks or so before she's born? I wouldn't like that."

"I wouldn't, either, but that's the way it is for her now. She doesn't have any choice."

"A lot of people don't," Sam said.

We took a tour of the hospital's labor and delivery rooms in Carson City yesterday. Then we saw a movie about a woman having natural childbirth. Two of the women in our group left the room when the blood began to gush as the doctor made the slash for the episiotomy.

Sam said, "I've seen freshly killed animals squirt blood like that when they're gutted, but I never thought I'd see a human being bleed like that."

I remembered him saying he let his first two wives take care of the children if anything went wrong because he hated the sight of blood.

"Will you be all right?"

"I'll be fine," he said. "You don't have to worry about me."

Charlotte told us to explore our feelings about the movie for our next meeting, but I didn't need to wait that long. I told Sam, "No one's going to convince me it doesn't hurt, that I've only been conditioned to think it will hurt. I watched that woman's face when the baby came, and she was in pain. All those blowing and panting exercises we've been taught didn't help her at all. You can huff and puff until your house falls down, and it's still going to hurt like hell."

It had been hell shooting in Mexico, even when he wasn't being fucked-over by the producers. Sam finally had to tell one who was a "candy-bar-eating prick" to leave or he'd stop shooting. All Bresler could talk about was money. Sam always wanted to do more and Bresler always wanted less so it was war all the time, until Bresler went back to Hollywood, then it was still war.

A climactic scene took place alongside a river near Chilpancingo. The water was yellow and brown, filled with huge turds, and you had to walk through a wall of flies to get to the river. You couldn't drink the water, couldn't eat the food, couldn't do anything but stand around waiting for the next scene, hoping you wouldn't die from the heat and the stench. People spent hours in the honey wagon.

Sam thought the men had to look progressively scruffier as *Major Dawson* progressed, which wasn't difficult, given the location, the circumstances. Their uniforms should be new when they started out, but they should be torn, hanging from them in shreds, tattered, by the time the film ended.

He remembered telling John Ford, "You know, they didn't have these perfectly pressed, picture-perfect uniforms in the cavalry." Ford laughed. "Yeah, but it looks great in color, doesn't it?"

He'd gone to the store to buy lettuce and brown sugar, because Kathleen had forgotten to get them earlier, although he didn't know why she needed the brown sugar ("The kind that pours," she'd said), since she was making enchiladas. He'd been focused—lettuce, brown sugar, M&M's, a red rose, maybe a good bottle of champagne, if he could find one—so he hadn't noticed Old John until he was standing next to Sam.

Old John and his wife had run the store when Sam and Kathleen moved to Yerington. It was across the street from its location now, and it had been called Johnny's. He'd run it for years and years but his youngest son, his namesake, didn't want to work that many hours, going on welfare, so John had finally sold the store. Now he was just another customer, a skinny man in his seventies with worn corduroy pants that bagged and a gray shirt with the tails hanging out. His oldest son managed a store somewhere in Louisiana, and his wife was a substitute teacher in Crowley. He never mentioned the son on welfare.

Old John said, "I saw your photograph in the newspaper today. I didn't know you made all those movies. I never met anyone famous before. My wife, she cut out the article, and said she's proud she knows you and the missus. She wanted me to tell you that. She's going to send the clipping to our son down south."

It made Sam nervous, being treated so differentially. He wished the goddamn paper hadn't made such a big deal about him and Kathleen moving here, but there wasn't anything he could do about it. You lived your life on the front page, if you were anyone at all. It was a balancing act. They'd praise you one moment and tear you apart the next, he knew that from his years in the picture business, but it was better to be praised than shit on. "Thanks," he said. "I'll tell my wife what you said when I go home."

Marion phoned them just before she and Elliot left Beverly Hills. She said they were going to drive up Highway 395 through Lone Pine because she'd spent so much time there with friends who'd shot westerns in the Alabama Hills.

She ran the largest movie memorabilia store in Hollywood and knew everyone in show business. She and Shelley Winters had lunch at least once a month at an upscale restaurant on Sunset Boulevard, even though Shelley always ordered hamburgers that were made with tofu and tasted like plastic, because she was constantly dieting, but she drank enough for three people. Eddie Dean had come to Marion's house, bringing his guitar, serenading her, and Ann Rutherford, who'd played Scarlett's youngest sister in *Gone With The Wind*, came over for tea each week.

Marion had frizzy blonde hair, and smeared her lipstick on. It was a vivid red. She always carried a large rag doll with her or a stick horse that played the "William Tell Overture" when she pressed a button on the back of its neck, and she always pressed the button. She didn't just come to a place, she arrived.

She probably weighed fifty pounds more than she should, but her boyfriend was a little guy with a scraggly gray beard that made him look Amish. Marion wore flowing dresses to hide the extra pounds, but no one cared. Sam had never heard her say a bad word about anyone, which was extremely rare in Hollywood. She liked to tell a story about the time Buster Keaton took her for a ride in his thirty-foot bus, wearing an admiral's hat, or another about Colonel Parker, before he'd managed Elvis. The colonel had painted sparrows yellow and sold them as canaries that had laryngitis. Marion was kind. She always kept her word. Everyone loved her.

Sometimes Marion would come to his house late in the afternoon after Sara had died. Marion would bring a pizza or chow mein and it was always good to see her because he didn't know anyone else who was that happy, but he ate alone most of the time and that was all right, too. He'd always go to the same restaurant. It was a small place on the Coast Highway, and sometimes you could see the seals playing at the end of the pier when the sun turned the horizon a brilliant red.

Sam always sat at the bar, his back against the wall, so there was only, at most, one person sitting next to him. He was uncomfortable when people asked how he was doing, he was doing badly, but the bar was a good place to sit since he could talk to someone if he wanted to, being simultaneously remote and accessible.

One of the women from the kitchen would come out with an anti-pasto after a few minutes, which gave him time to have a draft beer or two, and she'd look up and down the bar to see who was there. When she saw Sam, she'd smile, bringing him the salad, and say, "Here you are, Mr. Bonner," and he'd nod and say, "Thanks." Often, that was his most meaningful conversation of the day.

I made enchiladas, a garden salad, and an ambrosia fruit salad for dessert. Marion and Elliot brought me a box of miniature chocolates, which I didn't need, but I ate them anyway.

She said she'd only lived in two houses, both within a mile of each other, in her entire life, but she was as cosmopolitan as anyone I'd ever known. She bubbled on about everyone in Hollywood. She said she'd stepped on Gene Kelly's feet when they'd gone dancing, and she and Vin-

cent Price had gone trick-or-treating one Halloween. Everything Sam said about her was true.

He picked a tiny, delicate rose that grew on an arbor next to a picket fence in front of an abandoned house on Bridge Street. Someone said the woman who owned it was old and ill and in a long-term health care facility. The house was a pale pink and the rose was a deep red, and there were three gray and orange feral cats underneath the pine tree in the front yard.

Mason Valley might be the banana belt of northern Nevada, but the wind blew and raged some afternoons so it was like walking into a wall of wind. It was probably sixty degrees, but it felt colder when the clouds shielded the sun and the pines swayed and dipped. Then the sun would come out from behind a cloud, and the air would be warm again.

Sam had never felt more "right" holding hands, even in his late teens and early twenties when lovers were expected to hold hands, if acts of joy or tenderness were ever expected. He and Kathleen walked along Bridge Street, slowly, in the sunlight, the wind in their faces. He looked for another flower he might pick, but there were none.

I put the rose into a water-filled shot glass on the kitchen table when we came home. Some people might think Sam shouldn't have picked it, that he should have left it there to cheer someone else passing the pink house, but he said he wanted to give me something special on our special day. When I asked, "What's special about it?" he said, "I'm with you," the sawdust flying up through the sunlight in the lumber yard across the street as we walked into the wind.

They passed the Masini Ranch on the left, heading toward Wabuska. There were half a dozen horses grazing in the pasture next to some ornate out-buildings that seemed to be constructed of concrete and glass, along with a huge structure that resembled the Parthenon, although it was probably Italian in origin, rather than Roman or Greek. The early settlers had come from Italy. The Masini family owned Casino West.

Sam had heard some local residents complain about the money the family spent on the buildings, seeing them as a form of conspicuous consumption, what one person called "some sort of monument to nothing," but people who were poor often found something to gripe about when it came to the rich. Jealousy was rampant everyplace, not just in Hollywood.

"Why should they complain?" Sam asked. "It isn't their money."

Kathleen said, "Tearing down others makes them feel better. Bigger. It gives them a reason to justify their failure."

"And people think I'm hard on others," Sam laughed. "They ought to hear you."

Someone Sam had worked with said, "There ain't any halfway to nowhere," but he'd never been to "Beautiful Downtown Wabuska." The "town" consisted of a bar, which had been built in 1897, and probably hadn't been painted since then. It may have been white fifty years ago. There was also an abandoned house in the "town."

Wabuska had originally been a railroad stop. The tracks were so close the glasses behind the bar rattled when a train did come by, but that only happened a couple of times a week, and a train probably hadn't stopped there since Truman had been President. When one did go by, the barmaid would spin a large wheel on the wall behind her. If the number matched the one beneath the stool you were sitting on, you got a free drink.

Maybe all eight people who lived in the town showed up when a train came by, maybe it was their idea of a good time, but Sam wasn't even sure there were eight inhabitants. You could never tell in Nevada, since the city limits signs listed the elevation, but never indicated what the population was.

Sam ordered a Coors and Kathleen ordered a Diet Pepsi, and they both drank from the cans because the glasses behind the bar were dusty. They probably hadn't been washed since Truman, either.

The plaster had fallen away in swatches that looked like silhouettes of countries no one had ever heard of, but the bar was popular with bikers, according to the barmaid. Maybe one of them had kicked the plaster to pieces.

A bleached blonde with a sunburnt complexion showed the guy next to her the ring she was wearing. It glittered like glass. She said, "This is not real," holding her hand out. "It's not totally real. It's part real." Her red nail polish was flaked. "It gets in my way when I'm doin' yard work." She gave the word floozy new meaning.

It was difficult to imagine her doing anything more energetic than lifting a bottle, but life was filled with surprises. Sam knew that as well as anyone. Maybe he'd surprise himself and make another film someday, but he wasn't in any hurry. Right now, he just wanted to get out of Wabuska.

Sam and McQueen had argued about how the gunshots should sound when they were filming *The Heist*. Sam laid in one set of gunshots, but Steve wanted something totally different, and they'd almost come to blows in the cutting room. A lifetime of heavy drinking had affected Sam's low-end hearing, while motorcycle racing had wiped-out Steve's high-end hearing, and he was deaf in one ear to begin with.

When the soundman yelled, "Get the hell out of here, and let me do the job I was hired for," they stared at one another stupidly, dizzy from the heat trapped in the cutting room, then they went outside, laughing, their arms resting on each other's shoulders, into the blazing West Texas afternoon.

"I guess he told us," Steve said.

"I guess he did."

They cracked open two beers from a large tin tub filled with ice, wiping the sweat from their eyes, then they went to see Ali.

She'd moved into a mansion in Beverly Hills when she'd married Robert Evans. There was the usual pool, a projection room, tennis courts, terraced gardens, 26 telephones, and a huge black marble tub in the main bathroom. She and her husband slept on a king-sized bed paneled in calfskin. Ali said, "You have no idea how miserable I was."

"I think I do," Sam said.

"You have no idea how miserable I was," the letter began. "I made the mistake of getting married to Clark when I wasn't ready, and he even less so. I got out of that mistake, at a seemingly dear cost to you, mother, but it was my life. I wasn't going to stand for its ruination. So you don't care for the way I got out of that mistake--so what? There are a lot of things I don't care for, either--and so what? You keep saying, 'It happened. We have to discuss it.' Well, I went to the bathroom this morning, that happened, too, but do you want to keep hearing about it? These constant merry-go-round discussions, like the one we had on the phone a few days ago, are pointless.

"What was I supposed to do, stay in a marriage with someone I didn't respect or even like just because you approved of him? Do you realize we haven't had one conversation without your mentioning Saint Clark? Believe me, it isn't appreciated. It wasn't a marriage—it was a wedding. Now, with Sam, I have a marriage. That's a distinction you may not understand, but that's the way it is."

The leaves were turning amber and chartreuse as I walked across campus that autumn before Sam came to the university. People were making out on the lawn and laughing, and someone I didn't recognize on the steps of the library waved at me.

I hadn't slept more than two or three hours in that number of days, because my nightmares were terrible. I had a test to study for and a script to write for a filmmaking class, but I felt paralyzed, like Maria in Play

It as It Lays. If I'd known how to drive and had a car, I'd probably have done what she did, cruise at high speeds, but I didn't.

I stopped at a bar that was just off campus and ordered a glass of white wine. When the bartender asked what kind I said, "I don't care, they all taste the same," and he said, "What kind of an answer is that, do you think you're a comedian?" and I put my head down on the bar and began to cry.

He'd had heartburn for a week now and didn't like it because he wasn't used to being sick. Sara had been sick enough for both of them. He'd finally gone to a doctor who said, "You ought to be glad it's nothing serious, I see people who are dying everyday," but he wanted Sam to go in for X-rays.

Sam wondered why he was supposed to be comforted by another person's illness. If someone down the hall had cancer and he had a broken arm, was he supposed to feel better?

It was odd. Sam was leading an exemplary life, compared to the one he'd lead prior to Sara coming along, prior to Kathleen. Maybe the carousing had finally caught up with him, but he didn't want to think about that.

He sat on a green plastic contour chair in a narrow hallway that was too brightly lit, wearing a white hospital smock and hand tooled cowboy boots that had cost five hundred dollars. He'd bought them in El Paso.

It was probably between nine and ten a.m., but he couldn't be sure because the X-ray technician made him leave his watch, his wallet, his clothes, everything, in the bathroom beneath a sign that said *We Are Not Responsible For Your Valuables.*

He'd already had two X-rays and was scheduled for a third, and he'd just drunk a white, chalky-tasting liquid out of a Styrofoam cup. A woman in her sixties who was sitting next to him must have had the same thing to drink. She had a white smear on the lower right corner of her mouth and she told Sam, "I'm afraid. I haven't been in the hospital for more than thirty years, and that was to have my babies."

"What's wrong?" he asked.

"No one seems to know." She was wearing a white smock identical to the one he wore, but she had on a pair of fuzzy blue slippers, and the veins in her legs were blue. "Maybe it's just nerves, but I haven't been able to keep down any solid food for six weeks, nothing but fruit juices. Even water comes up. Even distilled water." Her blue-gray hair was stringy, and her voice quavered.

Given her condition, it was almost impossible to understand why she'd wait six weeks. He hated doctors more than most people, but he was ready to see one after a week and two Rolaids a day.

The old lady said, "My husband and I are pensioners so we have a fixed income, and our rent was just raised from one hundred twenty dollars a month to one hundred and fifty. And I worry because our granddaughter just moved to Kansas City. She's always been a good church-going girl, but my husband and I are afraid she'll fall in with the wrong people."

"I'm sure she'll be fine," Sam said, wondering who the wrong people were. He was glad when the technician told him to follow her down the hall for the X-ray.

There was a light snow on the mountains surrounding the valley when they awakened the following morning. They lay in bed, holding each other, reminiscing quietly. Kathleen told him how she'd made her first glider out of balsa wood, and how her kite wouldn't fly when she was a child. "The houses were too close together in the neighborhood."

They'd almost come to the point where they could read each other's minds, so they could go for long periods without talking, although Kathleen had always been quiet, probably because she'd had to relearn how to talk, how to form each syllable, after she'd been hit by the car. Sometimes, they would say the same thing at a given moment and laugh. Little things amused them.

He'd come home one Saturday afternoon as a Flash Gordon serial was ending on television. It had been made years before Kathleen had been born, but she talked, excitedly, about Flash doing battle with Ming the Merciless, and Sam remembered seeing the serial at the Kinema Theater in Fresno when he was a kid, remembered Flash battling the Lion Men, Gocko, the dragon-lizard monster, and King Kala's underwater aliens.

Their childhoods, despite the difference in years, were as similar as they were different. He'd had a kite, too, but his had twirled into the twilight when he was at his grandparents' ranch near Bass Lake. Both of them had played kick the can and exploded firecrackers on the Fourth of July.

The night before they'd watched a movie, hoping the bad guy, Walter Matthau, would get away and were pleased when he did, but Sam had always had a soft spot for misfits and losers, which was why he'd made so many films about them.

Kathleen laughed. "The next thing you know, we'll be sticking up banks."

"I'm too old for that shit," Sam said.

I was always crying that autumn before Clark was supposed to come back. It was the most beautiful fall I could remember, the wind warm, the sky effervescent, but that didn't matter.

I remember stepping on a nail and not knowing it because I didn't have any feeling in my left foot due to the cerebral hemorrhage I'd had when the car hit me. I remember realizing something was wrong when my shoe filled with blood and I remember my hands shook as I took the shoe off, sitting on the toilet in the bathroom, trying to put a band aid on, "Damn it, damn it," and crying.

I remember losing the wedding ring Clark had given me. I might have taken it off when I washed my hands in the bathroom of one bar I'd been to, or maybe the ring fell out of my pocket when I'd stuffed it there, although I never pretended I was single. I realized the ring was gone in the morning, remember back tracking my steps, as best I could remember them, but the ring was gone.

That time I didn't cry.

Sam told me to pack whatever we'd need for an overnight trip, but he wouldn't tell me where we were going.

"Let it be a surprise," he said.

"What kind of clothes do I need for this surprise," I asked, "anything fancy?" but he wouldn't tell me that, either.

I put a few things into a cloth carpet bag a friend had given us for our wedding and said, "I'm ready," and we drove north on Highway 95A until we reached Fernley, then west on 80, through Reno.

We had lunch at a small café on the main street of Truckee with its 19th-century false-front buildings and train station, then crossed the Sierras in the dreamy afternoon and I fell asleep until we reached Auburn, but I always fell asleep after lunch when I was in a car.

Sam stopped for gas on the outskirts of Sacramento and, for a moment, I thought we might visit some of our friends there, but Sam drove on, past Davis, past Vacaville, then headed toward Napa. I thought we might be going to one of the wineries in the valley, but we didn't do that, either.

We finally stopped before a jewelry store on the main street in Santa Rosa.

Sam said, "Wait here, I need to see a friend," then he went into the store. It all seemed mysterious. Why Santa Rosa? What friend?

When Sam came out, he handed me a small black velvet box with a solitaire diamond inside it. He said, "My friend knows more about fine stones than anyone I've ever met, and I asked her to find a suitable diamond. I thought it was time you had a new ring."

Of course he'd given her a ring earlier. They'd bought matching rings that were hand engraved in Sausalito on an afternoon when the sun had finally broken through the fog, but they still wore jackets. The rings had been engraved by someone who'd moved there from New Zealand to engrave gun barrels, but there was more money in rings.

They had a drink at The Valhalla, a bar and restaurant owned by Sally Stanford, and sat near the windows so they could watch the sailboats. She'd been the madam of a whorehouse that catered to the rich and famous who wanted to remain anonymous in San Francisco until she'd moved across the bay to Sausalito and become a different kind of entrepreneur. When they'd been there, Sally was sitting on a stool that resembled a barber's chair at the end of the bar. She'd asked Sam, "Haven't I seen you someplace? You look familiar," but her whorehouse was one he'd missed.

They spent the night in Santa Rosa, less than half an hour from her parents' place in Rohnert Park, but they decided not to call them. "Maybe next time," Kathleen said, and he was relieved. Thinking about them made him tired, tired of being called a four time loser, even though he'd only been married three times before he'd met Kathleen, and Sara had died, so he shouldn't be blamed for that. Maybe Kathleen's mother was lousy at math. She'd declared their marriage a failure from the beginning, even though Ellen didn't know anything about him. It was all tedious. He wished he could think of one thing he liked about Ellen, but nothing came to mind.

"Here's a cocktail for you."

One of the women who worked in the X-ray department handed Sam a Styrofoam cup. It was filled with some pink stuff, which he drank, wondering why everything that was supposed to be good for you tasted so terrible.

Someone who must have been eighty sat next to Sam. He was overweight and had gray hair and a walrus mustache and he'd been talking to a red-headed girl who must have been six when Sam came into the room. Sam imagined the guy had been born talking and never quit, but he was probably just lonely. "They have me in here because they think maybe I had a heart attack and didn't know it." Yeah, he was lonely, one of those people who blurted out his life story in five minutes. "I don't think these doctors know what they're talking about, though. Down the road, Dr. Pellegrini runs a clinic, and he's one of the best heart men anywhere. When I get out of here, I'm going to see him."

He leaned toward Sam, ready to fall off the plastic chair, as if they were conspirators. "I've been having heartburn, but I think it might be from chewing tobacco. I used to smoke, but the doctors wanted me to give it up, so I did. But I missed it. Couldn't seem to relax. So I started putting a chew in the corner of my mouth. Seemed to give me something to do, but I'd swallow it sometimes. Maybe there wouldn't be a handy place to spit, or I'd get absent-minded. But, hell, everything bothers me now. Cold pop or beer gives me heartburn.

"Down in Florida, when I go into a place, I'll tell them to give me a bottle of pop with no ice. If I have a beer, I'll wait for it to get warm before drinking it. If I don't, I feel it burn all along here," and he moved his hand down the center of his chest to his stomach.

"I like to get away from the winter," he said, "so I go down there, visiting friends, and play boccie ball."

Sam remembered watching old Italian men playing boccie near the Marina or in Golden Gate Park in San Francisco. They all wore dark suits, but sometimes they took their coats off, so you could see the black elastic armbands they wore at their elbows. Sam had no idea why.

"I'll be glad to get out of here," the old guy said.

"Me, too."

Sam's friend in Santa Rosa was 59, Jewish and had dyed reddish-brown hair. Julia had lived with an actor who was crazy, but most of the people Sam had worked with were crazy. He thought most forms of madness were a way to avoid life, but a lot of people had good reasons to go mad. Maybe madness was one way to cope.

Sam had cast Lee as a crazy person in *Borderland,* and he'd gradually gone crazy. It was a case of life imitating art. Sometimes it happened. Errol Flynn had played so many lovers on screen that he'd become one, although most of his "loves" were teenaged girls and got him into a lot of trouble, in and out of court.

Lee was Flynn's opposite. He didn't know how to relate to women, any women, but he'd pursued Julia, taking her to every bed and breakfast along the coast from Carmel to Mendocino, eating at fine restaurants, buying her champagne, flowers, stuff. She loved stuff. She'd sold a lot of it when she'd worked at Cartier's in Beverly Hills, which was where she'd learned about diamonds.

Sam had warned her not to move in with Lee, to stay as far away from him as possible, because he was crazy, but she'd just laughed, "Sam, you're the craziest person I know."

It was a point well taken.

Sam sat on the railing outside the community center. The break had probably ended, but he was tired of listening to Charlotte waffle about nutrition. He didn't feel like going back, but Kathleen would worry about him and she was worried enough already. She said it wouldn't surprise her if he had an ulcer because he'd pushed so hard so many years, pushed to make the best films, pushed to be famous, burning, hungry for everything but what he'd really needed: love. He wished he were home, doing anything, with Kathleen, even watching a rerun of *The Waltons.*

Earlier, Lauri's husband—Lauri, with her T-shirt that said BABY on it and had an arrow pointing toward her stomach—asked Charlotte if there were any evidence that smoking marijuana was harmful to the fetus, not that he smoked it, of course. He just wanted to know because he had a friend who smoked it all the time. He reminded Sam of a childhood friend from Fresno.

George had the worst case of pimples Sam had ever seen. He'd tried every non-prescription drug on the market and none of them had worked. George had finally gone to a doctor and said, "Tell me, Doc, I have this friend who jerks-off all the time. Will he get pimples?" It was pathetic.

Sam wanted to go up to Lauri's husband when the break started and say, "Parents who smoke marijuana have retarded children." Larry was retarded, but Sam tried not to be cruel these days.

Charlotte had tried to cover the subject of pregnancy and sex, but had made a mess out of it. She'd said, "Some people think that the, uh, closeness a couple gets from having sex toward the end of a pregnancy is, uh, a good thing. But other people think that, uh, it isn't such a good thing. I guess it's up to you."

Brilliant, Sam thought, really fucking brilliant, then he went back into the community center.

They'd gone shopping in Carson City after Sam learned he was all right, that there was no ulcer, no internal bleeding, no sign that anything was wrong. Maybe it had all been in his head. Maybe all he needed was a Tums, some Milk of Magnesia, a couple of laughs, a lot of love.

They bought more baby things, blankets, diapers, bibs, and a quilt for the crib at Penney's, then they went to the supermarket because there wasn't one in Yerington.

Standing in the aisle, canned goods on either side of them, he suddenly felt relieved, suddenly tired, he was actually all right. He thought he was going to fall for a moment, but took a deep breath, then another, thinking of what Dr. Casey had said, "Relax, then relax some more."

He hugged Kathleen, hanging onto her, while the face of the Jolly Green Giant stared down at him from the label on a can of corn.

I awakened from a dream at three a.m. because I had to go to the bathroom, but that's common since I became pregnant. My pillows were crumpled, the one under my leg was twisted, and the one under my head was smashed against the headboard.

I turned and swung myself into a sitting position at the edge of the bed. I felt in the dark with my right foot for my fuzzy green slippers. (I used to have fuzzy pink slippers, but I threw up on them.) Hooking my left slipper with the toes on my right foot, I brought the slipper to my hand and placed it on my foot, careful not to crush the toes. Just because there's no sensation in my left foot, doesn't mean it can't get hurt, it just means I won't feel it getting hurt.

I rose, took one step and leaned against the wall for a minute, till I regained my balance. I remembered my brother had been smiling in my dream, which was strange, because Jerry never smiled.

In the dream, Sam and I were in the living room of my parent's trailer in Rohnert Park. I was in the chair by the door, my mother was sitting on a footstool in front of me, my brother was sitting behind her, my dad was on the couch opposite us, and Sam was sitting in another chair. My mother and Sam had gotten into a heated discussion over Saint Clark and what she called my unorthodox behavior. Sam quietly got up and went into the next room to get our coats, but I could tell he was furious.

I told my mother, "We're leaving for good, is that what you want?" and she said, "No, of course not," then we embraced and both started to cry.

My dad smiled, and my brother told me Sam and I should come visit him. Then Sam came back into the room, holding our leather jackets, and everything was fine, family harmony had somehow been restored, but it was a dream.

My mother believes dreams are premonitions, most of the time, but she'll also say, "You dreamed that because it was on your mind." Her answer depends on the circumstances and on what she wants.

I believe you dream about the things that are bothering you. I dreamed what I did because I haven't heard from my mother in response to the last letter I sent, and I wonder what she'll say.

In the dream, my father, who's played an insignificant role in this conflict, was seated further away from me, and I'm not sure why my brother was even present, since his role has been almost nonexistent.

My mother reacted, in the dream, the way I hope she will, with an embrace of love and acceptance with no more ranting, but that will probably never happen.

Kathleen needed some nursing bras but couldn't find any that fit, none came with an A cup, but she finally got some regular bras that would work.

The models pictured on the brassiere packages at Penney's had their nipples air-brushed out, whereas the models on the bra packages at other, higher end shops showed their nipples. That seemed to suggest the women who shopped at Penney's came from a lower, less educated class or were, at least, more conservative. The people who managed Penney's must think their customers were hicks. Maybe most of them were. Kathleen's mother shopped there.

Sam sat on a chromium chair beneath a display of girdles near the dressing rooms, while Kathleen was trying on bras. Women coming in and out of the dressing area looked nervous when they saw him. They probably thought he was some kind of a pervert, but he just nodded and said, "Good evening, ladies," smiling, pushing aside girdles, as the women passed by.

WHAT KATHLEEN SAID TODAY

"I have a shape like Alfred Hitchcock's." (She was standing in front of the full-length mirror, looking at her profile.)

"I'm bulky."

"My legs hurt." (She'd taken two darvon.)

"Pretty soon I'll have skin over thirty." (A TV commercial for skin conditioner—Rain Tree?—made her feel prematurely old.)

"The yard needs to be raked."

"I don't feel like doing anything."

"I'm a pregnant dud."

"How do you stand all my complaints?"

"Have I told you I love you?"

"Things aren't going well, I heard the nurse," Sam said, as I came out of the obstetrician's office into the waiting room.

"I'll tell you later," I said.

The room was filled with women, either pregnant or with small children, and it smelled of perfume and disinfectant. There were some magazines with torn covers on a rack next to the door. The walls were peach colored and the rug a faded burgundy. Whoever designed the place must have been color blind.

Sam, as always, opened the door of the car on my side for me, then walked around to the driver's side in the cinnamon light of late afternoon. It was probably sixty degrees, so it was difficult to believe Thanksgiving was only a couple of weeks away.

Sam got into the car and looked at me, waiting. Neither of us smiled.

"I'm on weekly o.b. visits now. Casey's concerned about my ankles swelling so much, and my blood pressure is up a few points."

"How high is it?"

"Not abnormally. I asked the nurse, but didn't ask for a specific number. It wouldn't have meant anything to me anyway."

I could hear our breath until Sam turned the ignition on and headed south, past all the car dealerships, past the Highway 50 turnoff to Tahoe. There was a scattering of snow on the peaks.

"I also gained three pounds, which is two pounds more than I should have. That, coupled with the blood pressure and the swollen ankles, means I'm in trouble. Casey said he'll have to put me in the hospital if things

don't improve, but I think he was just trying to scare me. He isn't going to put me in the hospital for six weeks."

We'd stopped at a light just north of Minden.

Sam reached over and pulled up my left pant's leg so he could see the ankle. It was ballooned out.

"He certainly scares me," Sam said.

They walked past the Catholic Church with its tiled red roof, huge copper doors and stained glass windows. One seemed to depict Joseph, Mary and a young Jesus, and the other, smaller window might have a dove in it. Sam hadn't been raised Catholic, so it was difficult to tell, and Kathleen didn't care. The sky was cloudless and brilliant blue, and the cross on top of the church was stark and white. Sam said, "You shouldn't be on your feet too long," and Kathleen said, "I'm not an invalid yet," but they went home and slept.

When they awakened, the first stars had come out, but it was still light. The sky seemed milky. Kathleen said she'd broil steaks because a meal without meat wasn't dinner, but Sam didn't want her to stand that long because of the pain she was still in. Even her feet were swollen, not just her ankles. He volunteered to make the steaks.

Kathleen said, "Why don't you phone the Copper Canyon Café and order an antipasto?" The café was down the street from Casino West and Dini's, and the dining room was filled with pictures taken of the old mining towns—Tonopah, Goldfield, Eureka—during their heyday, and the names of some of the other mining towns—Austin, Beatty, Silver Peak--hung from the ceiling on wooden signs that were hand-lettered.

Sam remembered all the antipastos he'd eaten, his back to the wall, after Sara had died. He said, "I don't want an antipasto."

Dawn rippled across the hills like quicksilver, and Sam remembered other quicksilver mornings, one with Steve and Ali in a hot tub shortly after *The Heist* had wrapped, another in a swimming pool in

Boulder, Colorado after he and a woman he'd met there had made love and a drunken poet stumbled by, asking if they'd seen the meditation center, but in those days Sam was only awake at dawn if he'd been up all night. These days he and Kathleen were often in bed by nine or ten. He told people it had something to do with her pregnancy or with the light in the high plains, but he had no idea what had caused the change.

He remembered another dawn, running through some side streets in the valley with a friend and his pet wolf. The sky was filled with ashes because of all the fires in the hills around Hollywood that summer, and the sun was almost invisible due to the smoke. He and Jack ran with wet bandanas covering their nostrils, as if they were bandits in some movie Sam might make, and the wolf ran alongside of them, panting. They'd consumed a case of beer the night before so they ran to sweat out the alcohol and for other reasons neither of them could define, any more than the wolf could. Maybe the pounding their joints took, the accelerated beating of their hearts, made them feel more alive, or maybe they were just crazy.

He tried to remember times he hadn't been crazy before Sara, then Kathleen, had come along, but it was difficult, almost impossible. He remembered getting drunk on Spanish wine with a woman he knew in La Jolla, the stars shimmering above the ocean. Arlene got angry with him when he said the wine was as smooth as Kool Aid, but he wasn't the crazy one that night. He remembered sitting on his porch at the house in Malibu before the fire came and wiped everything out and his father died and his first wife left him, all in the same year, but he also remembered sitting on the porch with Sam, Jr. and Ellie earlier that spring, playing "The Streets of Laredo" for them on an ocarina. He remembered sitting on the grass with a girl he met one summer when he was a teenager staying at his grandparents' ranch near Bass Lake. He and the girl, Corinne, sipped grape Slush Puppies in the hundred degree heat, their lips purple, leaning toward one another and, finally, kissing, but that had been so long ago it might have happened to someone else.

They went into Casino West late in the afternoon. A man they remembered, vaguely, came toward them, smiling, his hand out. He said, "Hello, I'm Bob, I'm 93," as he walked by. Somehow, the continuity of it pleased them.

Sam ordered a dry martini and Kathleen ordered a small glass of chardonnay because you couldn't tow the line all the time. "It gets boring," she said. "A little wine never hurt anyone."

A bleached blonde with skin that looked like cauliflower sat next to them at the bar. She was playing one of the poker machines, staring at it intently, as if it might hold the answer to the riddle of the universe or, at least, tell her where she'd taken a wrong turn. She said, "The course of true love is never a straight flush," then looked at Sam, winked, and lit a cigarette.

"What was that all about?" Kathleen asked.

"Damned if I know," Sam said.

They kept the top up on the convertible, the heater running, when they went to the drive-in at the edge of town. A western with Slim Pickens was playing. Sam had worked with Slim in *The Heist* and another film he'd made about Billy the Kid so he knew how good Slim could be, but *Shadow of Chikara* was an embarrassment to everyone who was in it, not just to Slim but to Joe Don Baker, whom Sam had also worked with, and Sondra Locke.

One moment could have been interesting. The Band's "The Night They Drove Ole Dixie Down" was played over images of the South's defeat, but the scene didn't work because it was photographed so poorly. The film failed when it tried to be more than a story about disillusioned Confederates who set off in search of some diamonds that were protected by a curse and the director added a supernatural element.

Kathleen rested her head against Sam's shoulder, then put a pillow under her feet, but nothing did any good. She said, "I feel bulky, no position is comfortable," but there was nothing Sam could do about it, besides taking her home.

I remember making out with a boy at the drive-in when I was in high school. He worked at McDonald's, and gave me free French fries. It was great. When I asked Sam if he'd made out at the movies, he said, "I was always too busy trying to figure out why a picture succeeded or failed. I had no idea I wanted to be a director at the time, but I guess I should have." He laughed. "Everyone told me I lost out on a lot of hot sex, but there was always more talk than action." "Nothing changed," I said.

Cody had bit parts in two of Sam's films, but they hadn't seen each other in a decade, so Sam was surprised when he'd received the phone call. Cody and his wife were living on the Stillwater Indian Reservation near Fallon, an hour from Yerington, because Nila got a job there. She looked like what she was, an Indian, but she was striking: almost six feet tall with glistening black hair that came halfway down her back. She wore shoes with very high heels.

Cody had black hair, too, but he was older than Nila, in his forties. He had a graying mustache and brooding blue eyes, and Sam had no idea why she'd marry someone like Cody, but people probably wondered why Kathleen married Sam. Maybe Cody had settled, too. It happened if you were lucky enough to live that long.

Cody had become famous on the set of the second picture when he'd drunk a six pack of beer with whiskey chasers, then pissed on a fire hydrant while everyone watched. A lot of the crew applauded.

Cody said, "I bet this will drive the neighborhood dogs crazy. They'll be barking and whining for days, wondering what kind of creature did this," but Cody had always been untamed. It was as if he had to live up to the frontier spirit his name evoked or maybe, like a lot of people Sam knew, he was just crazy.

Nila showed Kathleen around the reservation while Sam and Cody sat at a round wooden table, drinking Coors, in a room that was too hot from the oven being on. They'd baked a pepperoni pizza.

Cody said, "Some of my liberal friends won't drink Coors because the company is supposed to discriminate against minorities, especially Mexicans, so their refusal to drink it is a political statement, but I don't care about that shit." He had a voice like the guy who played the radio announcer on *WKRP in Cincinnati*. "Those same friends wouldn't drink California wine, either, when Caesar Chavez was trying to organize the grape pickers, but I wasn't going to let them make their problem mine. My political statement tastes just fine. What about yours, Sam?"

"I think we should have another Coors."

A huge truck hauling a load of hay came down Main Street, but hay trucks were common in cattle country. Pieces of straw glistened, floating off the truck, raining down, raining down. It reminded Sam of an earlier, better time in Fresno, before the tract homes had been built, when there was still some open land. Now there were Wal-Marts where there had been ranches.

Some people he'd grown up with had stayed, but he didn't understand them. Maybe they hadn't noticed the changes--or didn't mind them. A lot of people went through life not seeing anything.

A woman in her twenties stood at the bottom of the steps in front of the post office. She wore a rabbit fur coat and gloves that matched, and she clutched a copy of *Awake*, as if it held the key to her salvation. Maybe she thought it did.

She smiled when she saw Sam and said, "Good morning," her breath hanging in the air.

He didn't like fanatics, religious or otherwise, but he nodded and smiled back and went inside the building as quickly as possible because he didn't have any patience with people who insisted the end was near.

I threw two pillows into the backseat of the car before we left the house. I had an appointment with Dr. Casey, so I wanted to keep my legs elevated for at least an hour before he examined them.

"You get to be chauffeured," Sam said, but I felt lonely, isolated, watching the dust trails my toe made on the armrest until we came to Wilson Canyon. Then I watched for big horn sheep. I liked to tell Sam I could hear their mythic breath. One of these days, I'd see one.

I fell asleep once we'd passed the place where we'd had our champagne picnic beside the Walker River, but I was tired a lot of the time now. It was as if I needed enough sleep for two.

Sam parked in front of Casey's suite of offices an hour before my appointment, but I was called into the examining room after a forty minute wait.

Nurse Stern took my blood pressure, and said the doctor would be in to see me soon. I was supposed to take off my pants, but she gave me a sheet to cover myself. She was the second person I'd ever met whose name so aptly fit her personality. I doubt that she ever laughed. The other person was also in the medical field, Dr. Stone.

Once she'd left, I waited another twenty minutes, naked from the waist down, dangling my legs from the metal table, until the doctor arrived.

"How are you?" he asked.

I never know what to say when people ask me that. All they really want is an "I'm fine" answer. No one wants to hear you vomited last night or that you're constipated. But when a doctor asks, is it a greeting, as it is for most people, or is it a real question. Both, I decided.

"Tired," I said.

'From what?" he asked, looking at the chart Nurse Stern had left. I could tell he didn't really care. "Your blood pressure is lower this week. Good. How are your legs?" he asked, lifting the sheet to look at them." He said something that sounded like "Hmmm," pinching my left ankle.

"It's slightly darker than your right. Is the discoloration ever more pronounced?"

"Yes, but not often."

"Stay off of them. That's the only remedy. That and cutting out the salt."

I'd told Sam I'd scream if I ever heard the "cut the salt" lecture again, but I didn't.

"Slide down," he said, "cervix exam," then he put on a latex glove. I automatically tensed my muscles when I felt his finger go into me.

"Relax!" He and Nurse Stern were really a pair. I doubted either of them ever laughed. I wondered what they did for fun.

He washed his hands at a stainless steel sink in the corner and said, "There's no sign of dilation. You'll probably go all the way to term, about the end of next month. Maybe you'll have a Christmas baby. Meanwhile, stay off those feet, young lady." He pointed at them, as if I might not know where they were.

He watched as I grunted and slid off the table, carefully, but every move I made was careful now. "I'm so tired of being bulky I'd happily deliver tonight. I know, it's great for the kid, but I'm tired of being bulky. It's even hard to tie my shoes," I said, but I could tell he was already thinking about his next patient.

Charlotte told the class Mary Ellen and Bonnie both had baby boys since the last meeting. Then she paused and said, "Fred and Paulette lost their baby. Paulette phoned me this morning and said she hadn't felt the baby move since Monday, and yesterday she and Fred went to Reno to see their o.b. and he told them he couldn't hear the baby's heart beat."

Charlotte paused again. "I wonder if Paulette and Fred will want to come to our class reunion?"

Sure, Sam thought. Paulette can come and look at everyone else's baby and bring her teddy bear. Sure, Charlotte, she won't want to miss our picnic. Paulette, who came to class because she said she was nervous, because she wanted to learn how to relax. This would have been her and Fred's first child. Paulette, who lay on her bed practicing her breathing exercises, telling herself to be calm. Imagining how she'd feel in the night when the baby was crying and she didn't know why. Paulette won't have to worry about

that now.

Don't look for me at the reunion.

He'd almost gone to his first high school class reunion. It was held on a humid summer day in Fresno. The palm trees in front of the hotel were blighted, the fronds clacking in the fouled air, and the light had drained out of the sky. The air smelled as if everyone in Fresno had flushed their toilets in the past five minutes.

Sam knew he was making a mistake before he made it into the bar. He hadn't liked many of his classmates, so he didn't see why he'd like them five years later, but he could ponder that while he had a drink. He was an hour early. He remembered the bartender must have weighed three hundred pounds, and his hands shook when he made Sam a dry martini that had too much vermouth in it. Sam thought about asking the bartender to make him another one, but it would probably be as terrible as the first so he didn't say anything. Maybe the bartender's feet hurt.

Someone was playing "Buttermilk Skies" on the jukebox, and Sam remembered breaking up with a girl while that song was playing. She had red hair and freckles and claimed all red heads were descended from the Lost Continent of Mu. He thought she was a little crazy, but he didn't mind the craziness as much as he minded her temper. He'd stopped by a bar to have a few drinks before picking her up for their date, so he was late. She was standing on the porch in front of her house, hands on her hips, when he'd arrived. "Buttermilk Skies" had been blasting from a portable radio, so she'd had to scream. She'd accused him of standing her up, but women were always accusing him of something in those days.

"Buttermilk Skies" was still playing when he left the bar, half an hour before the reunion was supposed to take place, and the air was even more fouled than it had been earlier.

He'd driven mile after mile with Sara when she was dying because it was one way not to think about what was going to happen, a way to try and ward off the inevitable. He'd driven more miles with Kathleen when she'd still been married to Clark, even when they had no destination in mind, *especially* when they had no destination, because it was one way to distract her and she was lulled by the movement of the car. She was still lulled so they took short trips, an hour, sometimes an hour and a half, away from home, because her legs bothered her if they were down too long, even though she kept two pillows on the car floor.

They passed Walker Lake, where they'd gone loon watching, heading south to Hawthorne. There was a huge naval base there, where some kind of underwater training took place. It was all top secret, but a friend said he'd gone past the base and the lake, holding a Geiger counter, and it had gone off. But Sam's friend had a fanciful imagination.

Sam and Kathleen stopped for lunch at a dingy casino in Hawthorne, but no place in town looked appealing. As they walked through the bar someone who looked as if he'd been sitting there for days told the frowzy lady next to him, "I'm drunker than a nine-eyed nigger." He leaned his elbows on the bar, trying to prop himself up, while the lady watched, blinking. He was skinny and had a gray, neatly trimmed beard and a red shirt with pearl buttons.

Sam had been with his first wife the last time he'd come to Hawthorne. They'd stopped at a thrift shop because Edie was convinced you could find "treasures" in them, although she never had. He'd gone to a bar down the street, because he was sure she'd spend hours there, searching, but she was sitting on the steps in the dust-diffused, cinnamon light, sweating, when he'd come back an hour later.

"You son-of-a-bitch," she said, "you abandoned me."

Kathleen made Cornish hens the first Thanksgiving she and Sam had been together. She served them with mashed potatoes, which she'd dyed blue.

Sam said, "They're beautiful," and tried to remember what his Thanksgivings had been like before he'd met Sara, before Kathleen had come to him, but they all blurred. He remembered one when he'd been a freshman in college and still lived with his parents and had come home drunk. It was late afternoon and relatives on both sides of the family were there. The men wore starched white shirts and ties and the women wore velvet, and candles were lit at each end of the table. He sat there looking at his plate for several minutes, then said, "I don't seem to be very hungry," and got up and excused himself. He remembered passing out, fully clothed, on his bed. By the time he'd awakened, everyone had gone.

He tried to remember a Thanksgiving he'd spent with Edie or Karen, any Thanksgiving, but nothing would come to him, although he remembered walking along a street in Hollywood the day after Thanksgiving, discussing feminism with a woman named Daisy Fields.

Sam had made a film titled *The Siege of Trencher's Farm* about a woman who was raped and possibly sodomized, and it had angered a lot of people, especially feminists. He remembered Daisy accusing him of being a male chauvinist, but people were always accusing him of something.

Sam finally said, "I'd have more faith in the feminist movement if most of the women weren't so ugly."

"Am *I* ugly? Am I?"

Daisy wore a short skirt and calfskin boots that almost came to her knees, and her brown hair hung below her shoulders. Even when she was angry, she spoke liltingly, elongating words near the end of her sentences. Talking about a movie she'd seen, she'd said, "I loved it *sooo* much," almost as if she were singing. He no longer remembered what the movie she had loved "*sooo* much" had been, but it certainly wasn't *The Siege of Trencher's Farm.*

He remembered a friend had come on the bus from Santa Barbara, bringing his Stradivarius, so he could play at a party Sam held for Edie, although he could no longer remember what the occasion had been. They were living in Malibu that year, and the party had probably taken place during the summer because the wind blowing in from the Pacific sounded like a person squirming in fever, it was a warm wind, and the crickets made little stabbing noises in the dark. You could hear them when John would stop between numbers.

They'd lit tapers on top of bamboo poles placed across the patio overlooking the ocean. The branches of a willow looked like purple smoke in the wavering light. Most of the people wore shorts or chinos and several of the men wore Hawaiian shirts, so the party took on the character of a luau.

John was in his early eighties and wore a black suit with a bow tie, despite the heat. It was a uniform to him. Sam had never seen him wear anything else. John had flowing white hair, and his hands, which had been blessed by the Pope, moved like an angel's wings when he played. Most of the songs were Irish and sentimental, but something had gone wrong about midnight or one a.m.

Everyone but John was drunk by then. Sam remembered Edie had thrown a drink in his face because he'd said something that offended her. He couldn't remember what it had been, but it didn't matter. It was just another day in their lives at the time.

They invited their new neighbor and his son, who was coming later in the afternoon, to have Thanksgiving dinner with them. Doc was in his mid-seventies and bald and he'd worked with athletes who were injured at a small college in Pennsylvania until he'd retired.

Doc had always wanted to live in the west. He said things like "whoopee" and "shucks," and he called Kathleen ma'am. Doc had learned how to use a lariat since moving to Yerington, and he had a pewter belt buckle that was the size of a dollar bill with an engraved long-horned steer on it.

Kathleen stood at the kitchen counter, getting dinner ready. Sam worried about her legs, but she'd reassured him. She'd kept them elevated most of the morning. She'd be fine. She was going to make stuffing and mashed potatoes to go with the turkey, but this time she wouldn't dye the potatoes blue. She asked Doc how an osteopath differed from a chiropractor, since they were both manipulators.

Doc said an osteopath could write prescriptions and was licensed to perform surgery, and there were more and more osteopathic hospitals. "The chiropractors are *just* manipulators. Everything for them has to do with the spine, they're glorified bone crackers, and they way overdo on the X-rays. Basically, they're all quacks."

Kathleen smiled. "You'd better not tell that to my chiropractor."

Doc's son had won a patient of the week award when he'd spent his birthday in the psychiatric wing of a hospital after attempting suicide. Kevin had been working as a guard at a jail in Worcester, Massachusetts, and he'd begun to drink in the mornings when he came home from the night shift after a love affair had gone bad.

Kevin talked about it breathlessly. "The whole thing came apart on Wendy's lawn one morning after too much booze and too many pills, I'd fallen apart gradually, then all of a sudden, and I was rushed to an emergency ward--that was before I committed myself."

Sam thought he was blasé about it all, but it had happened several months earlier. Maybe talking about it helped Kevin distance himself from the experience, or maybe he'd had too many beers. Doc had left after dinner.

Kevin had a scraggly red beard and blue eyes that were so fierce you could sense the madness behind them, and he was probably Kathleen's age. Kevin said he was thinking about entering a Ph.D. program in English someplace, but he wasn't going to rush into anything.

He certainly didn't rush home, Sam thought. It was almost midnight when he left, but he'd probably needed to confide in someone and, often, it was easier to talk to strangers than to friends. It kept bartenders in business.

They stood on their porch, watching Kevin cross the street, a dark, hulking figure in the starflung shadows, lonely, lonely, then they went back inside and turned off all the lights.

Kathleen asked a neighbor, "Where did your water break?" and Lil said, "In the hospital."

Kathleen asked a waitress at Casino West, "Where did your water break?" and Sheila said, "In the hospital."

Kathleen asked Bonnie, from their natural childbirth class, "Where did your water break?" and Bonnie asked, "Which time?" She'd just had her third child and a tubal ligation. The first time her water broke while she was at home, watching TV. She told Kathleen not to worry about her water breaking. "That's the least of your worries."

Bonnie didn't seem quite so stupid now that she was out of the classroom environment.

They stood talking to Bonnie in the neon light of Lyon Market. A grocery clerk with a dirty smock was stocking cans of Alpo in the dog food section. He was probably in his early twenties, but it was easy to imagine him as an old guy, sitting at the bar in Casino West in forty or fifty years. So many people led safe, predictable lives. Maybe there was nothing wrong with that.

Last night, they'd gone for a short walk. It was raining lightly, which was unusual in the high plains, and it felt like it might snow, but they wore warm, heavy coats. The streets were wet and there was the hum of tires in the dark when a car passed, the lights flashing, and a dog dashed across the road before them. The stars cascaded down the sky.

"I feel safe," Kathleen said. "No one will see my water break in the dark."

I haven't seen my cousin since leaving California. Lauri was a straight A student all through school and graduated with high honors from college, but she's unmannerly and lacks grace in everything she does.

Sam was with me the last time I saw her. She stood on my parents' back steps, her hands on her hips, like a roller derby queen, her cheeks blown out, and told us to leave immediately, even though it wasn't her house. She said I'd brought more than enough pain to my mother.

We'd gone to my parents' home to pick up a few of my things that were still there, not to see Lauri, and no one had asked her to interfere. But Lauri obviously felt she belonged.

Lauri's mother, my aunt who died of a heart attack, didn't like Lauri's choice for a husband, but Harry absolutely loathed my aunt. He called her a fat ass and always referred to her in the third person, even if she were sitting across the room.

My aunt was a very religious person. I remember her prayer every night once Lauri announced her engagement. "Please, Jesus, don't let me wake up in the morning. I don't want to see my Lauri married to him."

My aunt was a weak woman with nerve problems, and would have been happier if she'd died before her husband. But it didn't work out that way. Lauri's father died when she was nine, and she had to take care of her mother's fragile nerves from then on. She felt responsible.

I told my mother Lauri didn't have any business being there that day. My mother said, "Oh yes, Lauri did belong here then."

My mother phoned this afternoon and wanted to know how I'm doing. Just before she hung up, she said, "I may not understand you, but I love you, I want you to know that," but it sounded hollow.

Someone driving an old Plymouth passed us as we approached Truckee the day we left California. Its license plate read IM SAD, and the young woman who was driving looked as if she'd been crying, but she turned off the highway before I could get a good look at her, vanishing like a bad dream. IM SAD. It could have been me a couple of years earlier. It was the way a lot of people spent their lives.

They ate lunch, sitting on the bed together. Kathleen had fresh fruit--an apple, a slice of cantaloupe, seedless red grapes--and Sam had a hot dog with onions and sauerkraut, then they watched *It's a Gift* with W.C. Fields. He played a grocer with a nagging wife and kids who hated him. It was funny in places but, essentially, tragic. It was an allegory that said life was the shits and the only way you could hope to beat it was to stay drunk. Sam had tried that, and it didn't work very well. The hangovers killed you, and it was impossible to do your best work.

Sam drank two bottles of Coors, watching Fields, then he and Kathleen walked down South California Street, past the gleaming water tower and two story red brick elementary school with its cupola, past an elderly couple walking a greyhound that was black with a white tipped tail and feet and a grey snout, and he and Kathleen told the couple the dog was beautiful. He remembered Sara wanting one, but it was too late by then.

People driving by waved and smiled, even if they didn't know you. It brought back a simpler, friendlier time when the mailman came twice a day and sometimes stopped for a glass of lemonade when it was hot and people sat on their porches, listening to the radio. There was a station in Smith Valley that played some of the old radio dramas. Sometimes he and Kathleen would listen to *The Lone Ranger* on Sunday evenings. It seemed remarkable that the shows had been recorded before Kathleen was born, but he didn't dwell on that.

Some people were stuck in the past.

Sam remembered having lunch with an insurance agent in Petaluma. It had been a few days after Thanksgiving, and they were sitting on the deck of a restaurant that overlooked the river. Bud said, "It's a fall sky," but he was talking about more than the sky. He was going broke and his second marriage was in bad shape. It probably seemed as if everything was falling that afternoon, but Sam thought there was something bitter-sweet about the way the light hit the river as they looked out from the deck of the Fog Horn.

Sam asked if the quality of life in Petaluma was better or worse than it had been twenty years earlier, and Bud said it was worse because of the flatlanders, the people who'd moved to the east side of town during the past decade.

Bud had inherited the most successful agency in Petaluma when he was in his twenties, but it was almost gone and the past seemed a lot better than the future. His belt buckle had the name of the town on it and he was a member of the Boosters, but he was going under in the place he loved. Sam could be as nostalgic as the next person, but you had to know when to move on. A lot of people, like Bud, didn't.

The walks they took were shorter now, the rides shorter, and Sam would reach out for her hand, holding it, when Kathleen stepped down from a curb so she wouldn't fall, but her balance was always precarious. Holding her hand was nothing new. Sam just reached for it automatically now.

They stopped to watch a woman pick a rose from the arbor in front of the pink house on Bridge Street.

Someone had told them Mrs. Comet taught at the elementary school and was having an affair, but that was the downside of living in a small town, gossip, although people could gossip anyplace. Sam knew that as well as anyone. People in Hollywood thrived on it.

Mrs. Comet held the rose before her and said, "I'm going to take it home to decorate the kitchen table, so it will brighten Ed's day, he's been out of work for two years now," as if she needed to explain her actions. She was twenty pounds overweight and the floral print dress she wore probably fit her a year ago. She said, "I'd better run now, Ed will wonder where I went."

They watched her go, a frightened, aging woman in the winter sun, her life spiraling out of control.

Kathleen rested her legs on an ottoman in front of the couch when they went home.

They watched a rerun of *Tales of Wells Fargo* with Dale Robertson. Sam remembered writing some early scripts for the show, and Steve McQueen had guest-starred in one episode. None of them were much good, but one of the producers had given Sam an early break and Sam had hung out at his place. The house was two blocks away from Beverly Hills and almost as fashionable. Frank liked to brag about how much money he'd saved, but he liked to brag about everything. If you believed him, half the writers in Hollywood owed him their livelihood.

The house was a typical ranch-style structure, pleasant enough, but Frank's wife kept the drapes drawn and the furniture was covered with sheets. Sam's mother had been strange, but he'd never seen anything like it. Sheets were everywhere.

"Did you ever think about asking her why?"

"I was afraid to," Sam said. "There was something odd about her. She was very pale and wore a black dress that kind of hung on her and she wandered in and out of the rooms like an apparition."

"I didn't think you were afraid of anyone."

"You didn't know me in those days," he said. 'I was just another young guy, waiting for something to happen." He laughed. "Now I'm an old guy, still waiting for something to happen."

"This will be better."

"I'm sure it will," Sam said.

We sat, waiting, on the chromium and plastic chairs in Dr. Casey's office. The ship's clock mounted on the wall indicated it was six. We'd been there since four and had watched the sky darken outside the window, watched the limbs of the huge cottonwood writhe in the wind that came up most afternoons in the high plains.

A bearded man in his twenties sat across from us. He wore a Pendleton shirt and tan corduroy pants and leaned forward, staring at the door to the examining room. His wife or girlfriend had just gone in there. He said, "I've been here since two o'clock." He wasn't talking to anyone in particular. It was as if he were making a memo to himself.

I looked at Sam. "It's a good thing we both brought books."

I was reading Dr. Spock and Sam was rereading The Gypsy Moths. *It had been written by James Drought and made into a movie with Burt Lancaster and Deborah Kerr. Sam said it was originally supposed to star Steve McQueen, but the director had wanted to reunite Lancaster and Kerr after their success in* From Here to Eternity. *The film dealt with three skydivers, the third had been played by Gene Hackman, and took place one weekend in a small town in Kansas. Sam thought Frankenheimer had done a good job directing it, although one critic complained it was a study of nobodies going nowhere. You couldn't please all the people all the time.*

We sat there, looking at the clock, waiting.

I picked the book up, set it down again, crossed and uncrossed my legs, stared at another man who was waiting.

He had a gold earring in his left ear lobe and kept touching it. He had a dark complexion and might have come from Mexico or Madagascar. He said, "Casey stays with his patients while they're in labor, he did with my wife, for the entire eighteen hours. He's a good man." He sounded like someone giving himself a pep talk.

I pulled my left pant's leg up, staring at my swollen ankle.

Sam said, "Tell Casey your ankles swelled from having to sit all these hours in his waiting room."

I could get to hate doctors' offices.

Once on the grass he'd seen the moon between Kathleen's thighs. It had been summer in Sacramento and the moon was low, newly made, and she'd told him how she and her brother would break open tomatoes to clean the weed stains from their clothes when they were little although she had no idea why they'd done that. They were poor, but her mother had a washing machine, even when they'd lived in project housing, and there was always Spray & Wash. It seemed like an odd conversation to have after you'd made love, but maybe it was easier to talk about stupid stuff when your guard was down.

Now he could feel her restlessness as they lay on their bed in the moonlight that came through the shutters. She lay on her left side, sighing, on her right, sighing, then asked, "Are you awake, Sam?"

"I am now."

"Would you get me a sleeping pill?"

"Sure."

He went into the bathroom, took the bottle from the medicine cabinet above the sink and shook a pill into his hand. He filled a plastic glass with water and went back into their room.

He sat on the bed beside her in the moonshadow.

"Are you sure you want this?"

'I'm not sure of anything, except that I need you to hug me. Come back to bed," she asked, and he lay beside her again.

He and Kevin sat at the bar in Casino West. They were drinking Coors, listening to a country singer on the jukebox. It was another song about women and beer and wrecked lives, and he realized he'd had enough of wrecked lives, his own included. He'd been there, done that, as a friend liked to say, but the beer tasted good. He'd moved on. With Sara. With Kathleen.

"I thought my life was wrecked when my mother died," Kevin said. "I was in the eighth grade. I came home from school one afternoon and she was lying on the kitchen floor and there was a broken bowl next to her and cake batter all over the linoleum. I'd never seen a dead person before."

"I'm sorry," Sam said, thinking of his mother, of how he and his sister would try to sneak by her when they came home from school. She'd be lying on the couch in the living room, a damp washcloth over her forehead, with all the curtains drawn. If either of them made the slightest noise, their mother would ask, "What was that you said?" and look up at them, her face pale in the near-darkness.

She complained about backaches, her feet and hands hurt, her heart palpitated, her breathing was forced, and there were the headaches, always the headaches. The doctors could never find anything wrong with her, but she was absolutely sure she was dying.

Sam's life would have been a lot simpler if she had died when he was a child, but she was too mean, too poisonous. He thought about telling Kevin about her, how he'd thought about pissing on her grave when she finally did die and he was an adult, but he didn't want to seem callous, he liked to think he wasn't, so he said, "Let's have another beer."

She was sitting on the couch when he came home, twisting a white handkerchief into knots, and she was almost crying.

"I thought you were going to the post office," she said.

"I did, then I met Kevin and we had a couple of beers."

"I worried about you." Her feet rested on the ottoman with the embroidered turtles, and he remembered the woman who had given it to Kathleen loved turtles. "You should have called or something."

"I was only gone an hour."

"You abandoned me."

He sat beside her on the couch.

"Don't be ridiculous."

"I'm not being ridiculous."

"Yes, you *are* being ridiculous," he said, but he felt guilty.

The whole thing was idiotic, but he knew she was tired of staying home, tired of keeping her feet elevated. Tired of waiting. The last thing she needed was to be scolded. When he put his arm around her, he could feel her body tense, as if she were going to pull away from him, but she didn't.

She said, "Sam, oh Sam, I feel terrible," then she began to cry, and he held her more tightly, feeling her body convulse.

They lay beside each other on the bed. He wanted to tell Kathleen how beautiful she was, wanted to tell her how much he loved her. He was sure she knew, but it would be good for her to hear it, to be reassured. Some things couldn't be said too many times. "I love you." He said it over and over, softly, until she gradually relaxed and, finally, slept, and, still, he held her.

Lying next to Sam, I think about the places I might have become pregnant.

There was the inn where we stayed on the Monterey Coast. We'd had dinner and a bottle of champagne and we stood on the balcony overlooking the ocean. The horizon was cayenne red as the sun set. When we went back inside, we made love on a huge rug in front of the stone fireplace, the logs blazing, and I remember thinking we'd made a baby but didn't say anything because it was just a feeling, maybe it was the champagne or the heat from the fire.

There was the hotel off of Union Square in San Francisco. We had avocados stuffed with shrimp for lunch, then walked down Powell Street in a light rain. We thought about taking a trolley but didn't because I knew I couldn't move quickly enough, getting on and off, and it was fine walking, looking in all the windows. Sam bought me a carnation from a vendor on the street and wove it into my hair in front of a bar and grill with some fish in a tank in the window, then we went back to our room, listening to the rain hit the windows.

We drank a bottle of chardonnay and ate fried scallops while we watched the fishing boats come into the cove at Fort Bragg. The waiter brought us small bowls filled with a red sauce and another with tartar sauce. We liked the red sauce better, but they were both good. Later, we drank coffee at a small café off the main street and listened to a white woman who sounded a lot like Billie Holliday and who sang some of her songs, "What Is This Thing Called Love" and "That Ole Devil Called Love," and Sam tipped her twenty dollars. Then we went back to our motel. That time I didn't think we'd made a baby, but who knows?

He remembered walking up into some low tawny hills near Sonora with Kathleen. They passed a church with a huge white cross above the entrance and he remembered the sunlight glinting off the surface of the cross so that it had the look of a brand burned into the sky and he remembered an old woman they'd met saying, "Nobody is more important than God." Maybe she went to that church, but it didn't matter. He'd never understood God. They went back to the motel where they were staying on the main street of Sonora because Ben Johnson, who'd made several pictures for Sam, had stayed there. They sat on rocking chairs in front of their room on the small porch that jutted out from the second floor, watching the sun go down, then they went into the room.

They visited a small winery near the crest of the Mayacamas Mountains, then they drove down into the Valley of the Moon, where Jack London had lived. They passed a cow lying in the shade of a huge billboard that pictured a cow with angel's wings and a bow and arrow. There was a heart behind the cow and two other hearts with the words, CLOVER, *the only milk with LOVE in it* below them. It must have been around Valentine's Day. He couldn't remember, but he remembered making love in a rustic inn shaded by oaks somewhere in the valley that evening.

They'd stayed at the Winnedumah Hotel in Independence, 15 miles north of Lone Pine, because Roy Rogers, Gary Cooper and Bing Crosby stayed there, and Sam liked the sense of history—the continuity. Crosby was always given the room above the manager's suite so they could hear him singing in the shower, and Cooper came with his mistress, Norma Talmadge, on several occasions. Even

Gabby Hayes had stayed there. You could see Roy Rogers riding up to the front porch of the Winnedumah in *Under Western Stars*. He remembered Kathleen saying, "If it was good enough for Gabby, it's good enough for us," but he couldn't remember if that was before or after they'd made love.

It was almost dark when we got up. We sat in the sunroom, watching a cat walk across a neighbor's roof. The cat was a faded orange and its shadow was plum colored, and I wondered how it kept its balance in the wind, but I'd never seen a cat fall.

"I'm sorry I was so terrible," I said.

"You weren't terrible."

I felt as if the day had slipped by me somehow, as if there had been a hole in it. I hadn't been able to focus on anything, but I felt better now. More calm.

"What are we going to name the baby?" I asked.

"I have no idea."

"Maybe we should name her Sara."

"I don't know."

He got up, standing next to the door to the backyard. For a moment, I thought he was going to leave the room but he didn't.

"I think Sara would be a fine name."

"I'm not sure I want to talk about it now."

I got up, standing beside him, trying to see whatever it was he did. Maybe nothing. The cat was gone.

"Why don't you pour us a glass of wine?"

"Should you have one?"

It was the first time he'd ever asked me that.

"I don't think one glass will harm the baby—or me."

"I certainly hope not," he said.

He opened a bottle of Veuve Clicquot because champagne seemed like a better idea than wine. He could hear Kathleen say, "What a friendly sound," even though she was still in the other room, when she heard the cork pop, but it was something she always said when they had champagne.

He carried the bottle and two glasses into the sunroom, then poured the champagne.

"Cheers."

Kathleen said, "To Sara."

He knew Kathleen was trying to honor Sara's memory, but he wasn't sure he wanted to name his daughter after a wife who'd died, wasn't sure he wanted to live with the name on a daily basis, but they could talk about it later. There was always tomorrow.

"To Sara," he said.

He knew she was giddy when she started to talk about the places she didn't want her water to break. She hadn't said anything about her water breaking for several days, which was a relief. He was almost sorry they'd had the champagne, but it had tasted *sooo* good, as Daisy would say.

Kathleen said, "I don't want it to break at Lyon Market or the post office or the bank."

"Then we won't go to those places."

"I don't want it to break at the donut shop—"

"We never go to the donut shop."

"—or Dini's."

"We never go there, either," he said, and he began to laugh.

He half-expected her to stand up and put her hands on her hips in some kind of scolding position, but she didn't.

"It isn't funny, Sam."

"Yes, it is," he said. "You have no idea how funny it is."

It was three a.m., what Scott Fitzgerald referred to as "the dark night of the soul," when she pushed at his arm, repeatedly, awakening him. "Sam, Sam."

"Yeah?"

"A midget went to the hospital to have her baby, and the doctor looked at her and said, 'My God, you're *all* baby.'"

"Yeah?" He didn't know what else to say. He felt stupefied.

"Now *that's* funny. Don't you think that's funny?"

"I think it's hilarious," he said. "Can we go back to sleep now?"

I saw Dr. Casey this morning, and he was upset. My blood pressure had risen and my legs were swollen. He said, "Either get to bed and stay there, or I'll put you in the hospital." He wants to see me again in a week.

He also gave me an internal exam. I learned that my cervix is still tightly closed, so I'm definitely going to carry this baby to term. Cheers. My lower back aches constantly.

I can't sit comfortably because of my bulk. I can't lie comfortably for the same reason, and I waddle when I walk. That poor little midget must have been miserable.

My mother phoned shortly after Sam and I came home. I was surprised. She dreamt I had a baby girl last night. I told her Casey now thinks that it sounds like a boy. She said the same thing I did. He's playing both sides to be safe.

Casey prescribed a mild sedative for me. I understand why. He hopes I'll stay in bed more if I feel groggy.

He watched her put a roast in the oven. Outside, a light snow was falling, and the room felt warmer, somehow, because of the snow. Kathleen said, "I decided to make cinnamon apple rings for dessert, so I can use the syrup from them to baste the roast." He had never felt so domestic. It was something he would have ridiculed not too many years ago. Maybe he was just getting old, but it felt right, although there was no choice, whether it felt right or not, you got old or died. "Making my own spiced apple rings is better than buying them in a jar at the grocery because mine don't have all those preservatives that spoil the applely taste." He liked the sound of her voice, the way she said applely. It was sprightly. "The apple rings don't get mushy, the way they do when you buy them, because they don't sit in the juice too long."

"Why don't you let me finish up?" he said, although he'd never made a roast. He could tell she was tiring. "The worst I can do is fuck-up dinner, and we can always order something—or go out."

"I think I will lie down," Kathleen said. She kissed him on the cheek before she went into the bedroom.

He couldn't begin to remember how many times he'd ruined things that were a lot more important than a pork roast, two marriages, the children he didn't know, friendships, lost, all lost, but he didn't want to think about that.

They drove past the Yerington Creamery, which was the color of rich butter in the moonlight, and Sam remembered going to the creamery with his grandfather in Fresno during the summer. Milk was still delivered to your house in bottles in those days, so he wasn't sure why his grandfather went to the creamery. Maybe he liked the camaraderie he had with the manager. The two of them would sit in the back office, the fan going, and the manager always gave Sam a small carton of chocolate milk, and he remembered sitting on the concrete steps behind the creamery in the heat that was wilting.

It had stopped snowing now, but there was a fine powder on the cottonwoods along the highway and on the onion fields. He drove through Wilson Canyon, past the spot where they'd had a champagne picnic alongside the Walker River, past the turnoff for an RV resort they'd never been to and a sign pointing to the Smith Valley Baptist Church, and the little post office in Smith and a defunct bar with broken windows. There was a place that sold farm equipment, but it had shut hours ago.

Kathleen wanted a tree, even though Christmas was three weeks away. It was never too early to start preparing for "the holiday," as far as she was concerned. She'd been making a lot of her own ornaments since they were spending more time at home. She'd sit at the kitchen table for hours each evening, cutting out and gluing and sanding wooden paint-by-number ornaments, except for one she'd thrown away that pictured a family sitting around a table with their heads bowed, presumably saying grace.

Sam had been told about a place that sold freshly cut trees in Wellington, not far from the hotel that served Basque dinners. Maybe he'd have time for a drink before they found the right tree. Knowing Kathleen, that could take hours.

He put the tree into its stand once they got home, then they went to bed and made love, carefully, slowly, Kathleen on top. Sam felt the baby move, violently, just as he climaxed. He'd never experienced anything like it, although he'd felt the baby move before, when Kathleen would place his hand on her abdomen so he could feel it fluttering, but the baby hadn't seemed nearly so real on those occasions.

I remember going to Apple Valley with Sam to buy our first Christmas tree, a blue spruce, just before Clark was coming back. I was supposed to go away with him to Oklahoma and dreaded it. I told Sam we needed an angel to put on top of the tree so that it could watch over us, and I wanted it to stay lit all night so I could see the angel if I awakened, and I did, several times. In the morning I told Sam, "The angel guarded us all night."

Sam doesn't understand why I love Christmas so much, but he helped me string the lights on the tree this morning, helped hang the bulbs, and he put the angel on top while I sat on the sofa, watching, my legs elevated, and told him about a friend in Oregon.

"You think I'm crazy about Christmas. You ought to meet Joanne. She goes to a farm where they let her pick out the tree she wants, then cut it for her. She has them bale it because she lives in an old turn-of-the-century house with no double patio-type doors , and she likes bushy, tall trees that scrape her nine-foot ceiling and reach out into the room in welcome. Sometimes she'll choose the most imperfect tree she can find, because she

thinks of it the way she'd think about having a mutt that's the runt of the litter and needs a good home.

"The ceiling in the corner where she puts the tree each year is marred by the tops of trees past. One year, the tree actually poked a hole in the ceiling, and she just laughed and put tape over it, which was still in place the last time I saw her. The branches in back dirty the two walls they touch, and she doesn't mind that, either, doesn't mind the dirt and falling needles. She says it's as much a part of Christmas as the seasonal songs and she feels smug thinking of all the perfect housekeepers who'd have fits over it. Some of the needles under the rug are decades old, and she claims she'll be picking up needles until she dies.

"Joanne's decorations are cheap, old-fashioned dime store things, except for the miniature lights. She has a tin-foil angel with a mashed face that she got as a child. Sometimes the angel gets twisted so that it doesn't face the room, but she lets it stay that way because turning it is too difficult once the tree is decorated. It's a tree overdone with too many decorations and the icicles get tracked all over the house and cling to the furniture.

"She never uses a tree stand, but anchors the tree to four walls with string to keep it from falling, then drapes her Christmas cards over the strings. She keeps the tree lit all night and sleeps on the couch. She runs the TV all night, too, and loves to doze and then wake to the lights and sound of tree and TV.

"Joanne doesn't exchange gifts with anyone, doesn't attend church, but hosts family and friends for days. She says she feels like a better person during the season, even though she doesn't buy into the reasons most people celebrate it. She told her children that if she's ever on her last legs during the holiday, all she wants is a tree in the room with her."

"I don't think I want to know this lady," Sam said.

Soon they'd awaken in the middle of the night, and Kathleen would have to go into the next room to feed the baby. Or one of them would have to change its diapers. Soon they wouldn't be able to sleep in during the mornings because the baby would be crying. Soon they wouldn't be able to make love on a whim, because one of them would have to check on the baby. But it wasn't the end of a lifestyle, only the modification of one, Sam believed. What existed now would have new depth and meaning.

The baby seemed to move constantly, so there was the feeling they were being watched by the hidden stranger they'd created. Often, as they lay in bed now, they'd discuss the baby or the things they'd need for its arrival, they were always thinking of new things, rather than whispering (why did they always whisper?) the little erotic things they had in the past.

Instead of saying, "Let's make love," they'd say, "What kind of a mobile do you think we should put above the crib?"

Kathleen favored a buffalo, but Sam didn't think they made them.

He'd stayed away from Chinese restaurants for years because he remembered one he'd gone to in Stockton that was near the river. It was in the shade of a huge silo where they stored grain, and bits of grain floated in the air along the river so it was difficult to breathe some days. He remembered seeing a large river rat run across the slanting wooden floor of the Chinese joint when he ate there late one afternoon, and he never went back. He also remembered he had beef chop suey that was soaked in soy sauce.

Sam finally tried a Chinese restaurant that was close to his home in Sacramento. It had been years later and all his neighbors told him the food was superb, he should order the House Special with chicken, shrimp and beef, and they were right.

He and Kathleen had lemon chicken at The Pearl House on Main Street in Yerington, and it was very good. Her feet swelled from all the salt, but it was almost worth it. They both had the same fortunes when they opened their cookies: *You will have many bright days soon.*

"I like to believe that's true," Kathleen said.

"Believe it," Sam said, "believe it."

He remembered another day in Stockton one summer on the river. He was with a poet and his wife, who lived on a houseboat. They were in their sixties and as crazy and vital as anyone Sam knew.

The poet wore yellow swimming trunks, a Hawaiian shirt, a black beret and sandals. His wife wore a blue poplin skirt and blouse, and her long black hair was covered with a blue polka dot babushka. Her name had been Marie when he'd met her, but she'd changed it to Mariska in honor of her Polish heritage. He still thought of her as Marie.

Someone said it was impossible to get drunk on beer because you felt bloated before you got drunk. They'd been drinking beer all afternoon, docking their boat at every bar they came to, and they were all very drunk.

They sat at the bar at Rudy's on the River, trying to stay cool, drinking and sweating. There were huge overhead fans, but the blades just pushed the hot air around. They got up simultaneously, as if on cue, and trooped down a narrow hall that led to the bathrooms marked POLES and HOLES.

Mariska stared at the POLES sign, stupefied, then laughed, "Isn't that nice? They have a special one just for me."

"Pregnancy is a normal state of being," I recall a doctor chanting to me several months ago. Oh yes, so normal, always normal to have your belly turn red from the stretching, or to have your navel turn inside out, or to have to pee every hour, or to move so awkwardly, or to feel so bloated, swollen.

But complaining about being pregnant is like complaining about the weather. "This, too, shall pass."

If only I could be so blasé about the pain in my legs from the cold weather, but my legs have bothered me ever since I was hit by the car. I was given Last Rites four times. The doctors told me I'd never walk again and I said, "The hell I won't."

When I was making corned beef sandwiches for lunch, I dropped a pickle on the floor and began to cry.

It's the little things that are devastating.

Kathleen hadn't been confirmed in the church until she was injured. By then she believed God had saved her life, because everyone said her staying alive was a miracle. The people around her didn't understand all sorts of strange things happened and they had nothing to do with God's existence—or non-existence.

When her marriage to Clark failed so spectacularly, she lost faith in God and stayed on the pill. If he cared about her, if he existed, he wouldn't have let her get into something so awful.

Sam tried to tell her a lot of awful things happened, he knew that as well as anyone, and that they didn't have anything to do with God.

Hildy died this morning.

Hildy was a dime-sized fiddler crab I kept in a two gallon goldfish bowl. Sam got the crab for me yesterday in Carson City, along with three goldfish, two zebra fish, the bowl, some fake coral, some colored gravel, a box of food, and a no fishing sign. Sam thought it would cheer me up.

One of the zebra fish was missing when we awakened. We suspect the largest of the goldfish, Tector, sucked the tiny zebra into its big mouth.

Hildy wasn't named till we got her home (the lady who worked in the pet shop told me it was a female, because males have bigger claws) and dumped her in the bowl. She kept pinching the fanning tails of the goldfish.

I wondered how the crab would breathe, I didn't think crabs had gills, and the lady didn't know, either, but she said the ones she kept at the shop in a bubbling tank seemed healthy. I have no idea how you tell a healthy crab from an unhealthy one. I suppose I'll never know now.

It had snowed an inch during the night, enough for it to be beautiful, not enough to be a nuisance.

They saw two boys throwing snowballs at one another in front of the city hall, while someone wearing a sheepskin jacket stood at the top of the steps, watching them disinterestedly while he smoked a cigarette.

"I remember having snowball fights when I was a kid," Sam said. "We made red snowballs out of raspberry sherbet and threw them at each other, yelling, 'Gotcha, gotcha,' when we hit someone. Sometimes we'd be out there when it was a hundred degrees. We really thought we were cool when we were six or seven."

"What a waste of perfectly good sherbet," Kathleen said.

They could see the lights of Yerington as they came through the valley in the early evening, could hear the ranch dogs barking, then they were in the town, Kathleen more quiet than usual, pensive.

He drove down Main Street, slowly, so she could see the Christmas decorations: an illuminated Santa in his red suit, candy canes and wreaths. The wind was low, so was she, possibly. Coming to term could be arduous.

"I love all the lights, but it isn't exactly Los Angeles, is it?"

"Thank God for that," Sam said, but she didn't seem to hear him, didn't smile.

He turned down a side street, behind the court house. Christmas trees were lit in most of the windows, and some of the yards had Santa and his reindeer in them, others, scenes from the manger.

"Do you miss it?" Kathleen asked.

"Miss what?"

"Making movies, the fame that went along with that." She paused. "All of it, the whole deal." Deal and luck and chance were words you heard all the time in Nevada. They rubbed off on you.

"I don't miss the fame, and I certainly don't miss being called Bloody Sam. I don't miss being some fictional character the public created with smoke and mirrors. A lot of people thought I spent all my time whoring and drinking when I wasn't making movies, even when I was, *especially* when I was."

"Weren't you?"

It was embarrassing. He didn't want to lie, but he didn't want to tell the exact truth, either. He tried to laugh. "Maybe sometimes, but not as much as people thought." He doubted she would have liked him then, but times had changed for him, the way they had for some of the characters in his films. "I got lucky. I survived the catastrophe of success."

"I didn't know success was catastrophic."

"It can be. It can come at you in a storm of royalty checks beside a pool in Beverly Hills and you don't even know it, you just get on the phone and make another deal. People are drowning in those pools."

This time she smiled. "Aren't you glad I came along?"

"I certainly am," he said.

He remembered sitting beside a pool in Beverly Hills the week before Christmas. It was 10 a.m. and 87 degrees outside, and he re-membered watching a rat leap through the fronds of a palm tree. He was drinking his fourth or fifth martini, feeling a little drunk, so the young blonde women in their bikinis on the other side of the pool were blurry. He had no idea why the rat was in such sharp focus.

He'd been fired on the fourth day of a picture he was supposed to make with Steve McQueen and Ann-Margret because the producers wanted to make a "popsicle picture" and Sam wanted something with substance, since the picture was set during the Great Depression.

An article in the December 9th issue of *Variety* claimed, "Bonner's problems apparently stemmed from his filming a nude scene which wasn't called for in the script, but which the director wrote in on his own. Last Friday he reportedly excused the featured cast and began to lens the nudie scene using an extra from the cast." He particularly hated the phrase "nudie scene," but there wasn't anything he could do about it.

He'd filmed a scene where Ann-Margret was nude beneath the fur coat she was wearing but her nakedness was sensed more than seen, the bare skin captured on film was fleeting, and the scene wasn't about her. It was about the expression on the man's face who had picked her up for a good time, used her, and now just wanted her to leave.

In the film that was finally made Ann-Margret had a hair-do that was right out of the 60s and she looked like what she was, a bimbo.

There was a red telephone on a glass table next to the chaise lounge he was sitting on, but he didn't expect the phone to ring anytime soon.

I'm sitting in the kitchen with a cup of coffee, my hair in curlers, and I'm wearing a baggy sweatshirt, the light from my diamond ring reflected on the walls, the ceiling, the cabinets. The light moves as I do, until it rests on the angel on the tree top.

I can feel the baby kicking for her freedom, stopped by her body and my own. Soon baby, soon: two weeks, maybe three, and you'll be ready. I, too, am tiring. Weary of this stranger I carry in my womb.

The angel glows.

He remembered seeing two cops standing over someone in the dark in Sherman Oaks or Encino or one of those towns that were indistinguishable from each other in the valley. It was the winter he'd been fired from the Ann-Margret movie, and it must have been after two a.m. because the bar he'd been in had closed.

The cops were in a park across the street from the bar, and the person they were standing over lay on a bench. One of the cops kept hitting the person's shoes with a nightstick while his partner watched. It all seemed very clinical to Sam.

The other cop said, "Harder! You ain't hitting him hard enough," so the first cop hit the guy again, harder.

"He's dead to the world."

"Maybe he *is* dead."

The cops dragged him across the grass to the sidewalk, then stood there, staring at his body, as if they might urinate on it. They might have been maniacs.

The man's shirt had come out of his pants, so Sam could see his belly, which was very white. He was as thin as a stick figure, and he was very dead.

He knew how the cops in and around Los Angeles did business and it was ugly.

They were still standing over the body when he left.

They lay on a heavy blanket beside the Christmas tree, holding each other, listening to Dean Martin sing "Baby, It's Cold Outside." Maybe it was. They hadn't been out in hours. Sam was sure she'd be more comfortable in bed, but Kathleen wanted to lie next to the tree so she could see the angel on top. He'd taken the blanket he'd bought in Mexico out of the bedroom closet, spreading it carefully, as if it might tear, although it was practically indestructible, made by a master artisan.

Somehow, the angel was reassuring to Kathleen. She seemed to believe in angels, even though she didn't believe in God, which didn't make much sense, but a lot of things didn't make any sense. Maybe the angels hadn't failed her when she'd been hit by the car and God had. That didn't make any sense, either.

When Dean began to croon "I've Got My Love to Keep Me Warm," Kathleen asked, "Did you ever meet Dino?" He was her favorite singer.

"We'd pass each other in bars sometimes, both probably drunk, or in restaurants, but we never really said anything. We just nodded."

"Did you know Tom Mix was his favorite actor when Dino was a child in Steubenville? He dreamed of sitting around a camp fire with Tom, having a spaghetti dinner."

"Wouldn't that have been something? It's too bad they never got to do it," Sam said, then Dean began to sing "Blue Christmas."

Kathleen worried her water would break on the way to Lovelock, the sky brilliantly blue, the wind wild. Huge tumbleweeds blew across the open range. Sam had put one in a box and sent it to a friend in England, who'd only seen them in the movies. Sam's friend had taken it into his backyard on a windy day, it was always windy in England, Sam knew because he'd made a movie there, and his friend said it "worked," tumbling along beautifully.

Sam said, "It's only two hours away. We shouldn't let love pass us by."

"We can go there later, after the baby."

There was always later, he knew that, but he said, "We can't stay beside the Christmas tree forever, listening to Dean croon."

"Why not? I like listening to Dino."

Some things were imponderable.

Lovelock had become the nation's official love-locking destination. The town had adopted the ancient Chinese custom of symbolically locking one's love on a never-ending chain, well, almost never-ending. The people who thought it up claimed that as long as the lock remained on the chain, your love would endure.

Sam knew it was corny, a publicity gimmick, but he said, "It sounds good to me."

They bought a small padlock at the Chamber of Commerce, which was on the main street, the dust blowing, the sky almost chartreuse now.

The lady who sold them the lock had short-cropped gray hair and her shoulders were stooped. She was probably 75, and looked as if she'd never been kissed. She engraved Sam and Kathleen on one side of the lock. Lovelock, Nevada was engraved on the other side.

She said, "No one knows how or when the custom began, but the lock-laden chains, common in the Yellow Mountains and at the Great Wall of China, have begun to appear elsewhere in the world. Thousands of simple metal locks adorn chains and fences."

The lady was vague about where those places were, they probably hadn't been written into her script, but she smiled and said, "You can attach your lock to the chains in the park next to the only round courthouse in use in America." She gave them two keys for the lock and said they were supposed to throw them away so the lock would unite their love for eternity.

"It sounds good to me," Kathleen said. "We'll throw the keys into the Truckee River the next time we're in Reno," then she and Sam walked along the street in the rising dust to the park.

The Casino West lounge was filled with tourists from Merced and Madera and other towns in the Central Valley in California. The tourists got a package deal and came on a bus provided by the casino. They were generally in their sixties or seventies and went to bed early so the singer came on stage at six each Sunday.

He wore a Santa hat and was standing beside an artificial Christmas tree, and there was a red spotlight on him so he looked flushed. Maybe he'd had too much to drink before coming on. The song dealt with a crippled singer's blood on the snow at the blood-red close of day, which didn't seem very appropriate to the season, but this was Nevada. Anything went. Sam noticed he limped as he moved across the stage.

Sam and Kathleen headed through the bar toward the restaurant when they saw an old guy with his hand extended approach them.

Sam smiled. "You're Bob, and you're 93."

"How do you know?" Bob asked.

They stood on the bridge in downtown Reno, the same bridge Marilyn Monroe had stood on when she was making *The Misfits* and staying at the nearby Mapes Hotel. Sam and Kathleen wore sheepskin coats, because it was cold with the wind blowing along the Truckee River. There were colored lights all up and down Virginia

Street, along with the blinking neon signs that were always in front of the casinos. It was a neon wilderness.

People had come to Nevada because they could get a divorce in six weeks once they established residency, and it was almost impossible to get one in some states during the 50s and 60s. It was still almost impossible in some of those places, and Sam wondered why anyone lived in them. The weather was bad, the laws repressive, the people anal-retentive. You wanted to put the car on automatic pilot and shut your eyes when you drove through most of the Midwest.

Sam had been told there was more gold in the Truckee River than there had been in a lot of the boom towns, because the women who came to Reno to get a divorce would throw their wedding rings into the water. Maybe his first two wives had done that. He'd never asked, and it didn't matter now.

Kathleen handed him one of the keys from Lovelock and said, "You go first," and he threw the key as if he were casting for trout, the river was full of them at times, and watched it glisten and disappear, then Kathleen threw her key, the way a girl would throw a ball.

"Now," she said, "let's hope we make it home before my water breaks."

Sam said they had to have dinner someplace so they stopped at the Liberty Belle, a couple of miles south of the bridge on Virginia Street. They'd had dinner there the first Christmas Eve they'd been together. The proprietor's grandfather had invented the three most popular slot machines used in the casinos, and he was very proud of that.

The bartender wore a white shirt, a string tie and a black leather vest, and he was probably in his early forties. He could have been an extra in one of Sam's films, and he made an excellent dry martini. He put a couple of drops of vermouth into a chilled glass, swirled it, then flicked his wrist, flinging the vermouth into the stainless steel sink behind the bar. He filled the glass with gin, neither stirring nor shaking it, then he added a single green olive. It was a virtuoso performance and as perfect as anything in this world.

When they left the bar, Sam and Kathleen sat in the same booth they had that first Christmas Eve. He remembered someone dressed as Santa sat in the booth next to theirs, along with a cowboy who had gnarled fingers. He wore a red shirt and a huge black Stetson, and he nodded, grinning, when Kathleen said, "You must be the reindeer wrangler."

Santa looked at Kathleen and winked, his voice booming. "I ordered the prime rib, because I have a lot of miles to cover tonight."

Sam had a second martini before their meal came, then he ordered half a carafe of chardonnay. He poured some for Kathleen when she said, "A glass won't hurt me or the baby and a small toast would be nice. To us," then she held her glass up, touching his, before she took a drink. She surprised him when she added, "Besides, it tastes so fucking good." She almost never swore.

He thought about what he might give her for Christmas. He could give her candles scented with frankincense and myrrh, but she disliked the fragrance of incense or scented candles. He could give her a painting he'd seen of a cowboy who was standing on a white verandah holding a gold-colored sword, although he had no idea why a cowboy would own a sword of any color. He could give her a wind chime made with small pieces of silver that were shaped like buffalo, but the wind in the high plains blew too swiftly and too often for the sound to be soothing. He wanted to give her something that would indicate how much he loved her, but he couldn't imagine what that might be. He remembered her saying she wanted a husband who would rise from the table and draw his sword and with one sweep decapitate an intruder and place his head beside that of the boar on the buffet table, but that didn't seem very practical.

He settled on a necklace made from the finest Czechoslovakian crystal with matching earrings that he discovered in a jewelry store in Reno. They were designed by someone in New Hope, Pennsylvania and the card that came with them read, *These glass prisms were made in the town of Gablonz, Czechoslovakia by skilled artisans. The Second World War destroyed their industry and the emigration of the glass workers after the war scattered their skills. The ancient tradition destroyed, these prisms are the final existing relics of an historic cottage industry.* He was not only giving Kathleen something rare and beautiful, he was giving her a piece of history. It seemed a perfect gift.

Kathleen answered the phone the way she always did, "Yes," when it rang. She was silent for several seconds, listening, then she said, "I *am* being careful, mom. And Sam's doing everything he can to be helpful," then she paused again. "It should only be a couple of more weeks. It would be nice if you and dad could come here after the baby's born." She rested her elbows on the kitchen table, where she'd placed the phone. She sighed. "Yes, I understand how bad the weather can be crossing the Summit during the winter. I know how it is."

He stopped listening after that, but he watched her sitting at the kitchen table next to the window with the drawn white curtains that were as soft as the touch of love. The kitchen lights were off, but there was the light from the colored bulbs and the angel on the Christmas tree.

It was easy to imagine Kathleen's mother. She was pacing the trailer in Rohnert Park. She held the phone to her right ear with one hand and covered her left ear with the other so she could block out the sound of the television because her husband never turned it off. He was watching Jimmy Stewart or John Wayne or Randolph Scott shoot it out for the thousandth time.

Mrs. Jewell was probably telling Kathleen Sam was going to throw her out in the snow, because that was one of her favorite topics. She'd told Kathleen that right after she'd left her first husband, and Kathleen's mother was one of those people who couldn't be wrong. She almost never changed her mind.

She was beginning to shout now. He could hear her voice rising, even though he couldn't make out what she was saying. At least that was something to be thankful for.

The sky had the color and texture of porridge, holding back the light, so the hills seemed faded. They were on their way to Fallon to shop for more things the baby might need and to have lunch, although there didn't seem to be a decent restaurant in the town. Despite the presence of the Top Gun Naval Base, maybe because of its presence, there was something forlorn about Fallon. It had all the appeal of a boom town that had busted, although Sam didn't know if it had ever boomed.

There were some nice two story homes that had been built at the turn of the century before you came to the town. The homes had huge porches where the people sat outside during the summer in the shade of the apple and poplar trees and laughed and told stories the way people used to do. And there were huge red barns filled with hay and cattle in the fields.

They passed some cattle being herded down a side road before they came to the town. Cars had stopped so the cattle could go around them, and Sam remembered another day when he and Kathleen had taken a wrong turn on the way to Sierraville and were caught in the middle of a cattle drive. They had to stop the car, sitting there with the windows rolled up, as cows the size of the Cadillac surged by, their noses dripping. They were followed by three dogs and a cowgirl who crooned "Ki-yi-yay," swinging her lariat.

This time there were no dogs and two cowboys, but not much had changed.

Kathleen smiled. "The Old West lives."

"Yes. Isn't it grand?" Sam said.

He watched her cutting open small plastic bags with tilapia in them. Neither of them liked fish, but it was supposed to be good for you. He'd spent most of his life doing things that weren't good for him, but times changed. He probably still drank more than he should, but no one was perfect. It was funny what you did when you got older.

Kathleen thought the recipe sounded interesting. You mixed the fillets with two tablespoons of butter, a teaspoon of lemon juice, then broiled them for two minutes on each side. Then you sprinkled the fillets with sesame seeds and broiled them for another minute or two.

Each bag weighed about a third of a pound, and Kathleen was opening the third one when the knife slipped and she cut her finger. The cut probably wouldn't have been so bad if she hadn't sharpened the knives the week before, but her finger kept bleeding.

"Shit," she said, "shit," but she didn't cry the way she had when she'd dropped the pickle.

He stood beside her at the sink. They ran cold water over her finger, then blotted it with a paper towel. Then they ran more water over her finger and blotted it again, but the bleeding hadn't slowed down by the time they were on the third paper towel.

"I think we'd better get you to the emergency room," Sam said.

The hospital was six blocks from their house, and it was a one story structure made out of stucco. A sign in red letters indicated where the emergency room entrance was. The place had all the charm of a Salvation Army mission.

Two guys in their twenties sat in the waiting room next to some double doors that led into the area where patients were treated. They were talking about something that had happened in Tennessee or Georgia or Pennsylvania. It wasn't clear to Sam.

There was a television in one corner of the room, but it wasn't on.

Sam watched Kathleen fill out the paperwork she needed, then he followed her through the double doors into a room with two beds.

Someone who'd fractured his shoulder sat on one of the beds, and the nurse told Kathleen to sit on the other until the doctor arrived.

He was probably in his late thirties or early forties, and he was from India. His last name was Narwan, and he talked in a kind of bebop. He had her soak her finger in some kind of antiseptic before examining it.

"Yep, with that much raw tissue showing, we have to stitch it," he said, then he left the room.

Sam and I sat there, waiting. We could hear the guy who'd injured his shoulder moaning, but couldn't see him because a curtain was drawn around his bed.

I told Sam, "I'm really proud of myself. I remembered to turn the oven off before we left."

Sam said, "I'm always proud of you. I wouldn't have thought about the oven," then he got up from the chair next to the bathroom and went out into the hall. I could see him standing in the doorway. I kept waiting for the door to shut, the way it had at the end of The Searchers *with John Wayne, but it didn't.*

I thought about other hospital rooms I'd been in, other stitches I'd endured. I remembered the one where I'd been in a coma for nine weeks and another where I'd been when I fell off a bicycle and broke my leg for the third time when I was married to Clark. I'd had six stitches beside the lower left corner of my lip and eighteen on my right knee after I'd been hit by the car. None of it was very pleasant. Neither was the rehab center where they'd sent me, but they did teach me how to talk and walk again. It was also where I'd learned to smoke, which made absolutely no sense, but, as Sam observed, a lot of things didn't. I'd finally quit.

Sam disappeared from sight, but came back a few minutes later. He said, "The nurse assured me you'll be out of here in fifteen, twenty minutes." He said he could pick up some Chinese food to go while I waited. He'd be back by the time I was done.

He kissed me on the cheek and left, and I sat on the edge of the bed, waiting some more, listening to the guy moan. He let me know he was in pain and I resented it. He was showing off because he had an audience.

When Dr. Narwan came back, he put two stitches into my finger, looked at me, smiled, and said, "You're all baby, little lady."

"Tell me something I don't know," I said.

They opened the fortune cookie when they'd finished eating. Their fortune read, *Be yourself, and you will always be in fashion.*

"I wish I believed that," Sam said.

"I imagined you would."

They sat on the couch near the woodstove in the front room. It wasn't cold enough to build a fire yet, but it was comforting to know it was there when they'd need it.

"I fell out of fashion more times than I can count," Sam said.

"But you came back." Kathleen smiled. "People still go to see the films you made."

True enough. Sometimes one's honesty and effort prevailed over one's weariness and negativity, and something that resembled art occurred, even to the least of them.

"That's because I've been gone so long people think I'm dead."

"I don't think it's quite that simple," Kathleen said, then she leaned against his shoulder in the light from the angel.

Dr. Casey wants me to go into the hospital the day after Christmas because I have a condition that could lead to toxemia. "I'd put you in now," he said, "but it's only three days and I don't think anyone wants to spend Christmas in the hospital."

Casey looked at Sam, who was sitting next to me, and said, "I want your wife in the hospital so her diet can be controlled, so she can have strict bed rest, and I can have some tests run. I think her pelvis may be out of alignment. I want to have it X-rayed so I can see if there's sufficient room for a normal delivery. I might have to perform a Caesarean."

'How long will I be in?" I asked.

"That depends," he said.

"On what?"

"On whether or not I perform a Caesarian, induce labor or you have a natural birth."

"What's the worst scenario?"

"Three to five days, but you have to understand this isn't an exact science."

"I can't tell you how reassuring that is," I said.

He watched her pack the blue leather suitcase he'd bought at an exclusive shop he couldn't remember the name of on Rodeo Drive.

They'd opened their presents earlier that evening, after they'd finished dinner. He'd given her the crystal necklace and earrings, and she'd given him one of the original posters from the movie he'd made about Billy the Kid. His first or second wife had torn up the one he'd had, but he didn't want to think about that.

He knew Kathleen wouldn't be in the hospital longer than five days and that he'd be able to visit her each day, but he also knew how empty the house would seem without her. He didn't want to think about that, either.

Kathleen said, "I haven't gone yet."

He sipped a martini in the soft, colored lights from the Christmas tree after she'd finished packing and sat beside him, resting her right hand between his legs. These days he took comfort in small things, in the few simple ideas and few simple feelings he tried to be faithful to. He had no idea how he'd survived all those years in Hollywood.

Kathleen said, "I'm sorry Christmas Eve wasn't all it might have been."

"It's fine," Sam said. "I've had a lot worse."

He remembered the Christmas Eve he'd had measles. He was twelve and had a one hundred two degree temperature, and he was sure he was going to die. Everything ached. His parents kept him in a darkened room, and he remembered lying in bed, listening to *The Lone Ranger*. He also remembered having a fight with his first wife one Christmas Eve, although he couldn't remember what he and Edie had fought about. He remembered waking up on the couch on Christmas Day. He had a bloody nose and he felt like he was going to vomit, and the sun looked like the yolk of a bad egg. The sky was a sickly yellow. He went into the kitchen and made himself a Bloody Mary, but he still felt nauseous. All he'd succeeded in doing was getting drunk again, which wasn't an unusual story in those days.

He removed the stitches from her finger with a small pair of scissors on Christmas morning while they sat at the kitchen table, then he got out the number four coffee filters from the cupboard above the stove and the large can of Colombian coffee. Then he put the kettle of water on a back burner and waited. He'd already backed the car out of the garage, leaving it in the driveway, even though they didn't plan to go anyplace. He thought the phone might ring, although he had no idea who might call, perhaps one of his children or Kathleen's mother, but he didn't really expect that. He unlocked the front door and picked up the *Reno Gazette-Journal* from the sidewalk and took it into the house. Then he poured the boiling water into the coffeemaker. Sometimes the little things sustained you. Kathleen was still sitting at the table, wearing her fuzzy blue bathrobe with the hood. Sam said, "Merry Christmas."

They walked into the wind, slowly, on Bridge Street, holding hands. There was some snow on the hills surrounding the town, but the sidewalks and roads were dry.

Kathleen wore the necklace and earrings he'd given her because she wouldn't be able to wear them in the hospital, although they'd been careful not to mention the hospital all day. Kathleen had baked chocolate chip cookies so the house would smell good, as if the aroma would alleviate her absence.

She'd been reading Dr. Spock for a month and said he claimed boys worried about something happening to their penises between the ages of one and three.

"Did you worry?" she asked.

"Damned if I know. That was such a long time ago."

Sam stopped before a house with a brilliantly lit tree with a gold spire on top. He could see his breath in the air. "God, I'm going to miss you."

"Yes, but I'm coming back," Kathleen said.

He drove her to the hospital in Carson City in the morning.

If the baby didn't arrive by the 29th, Casey said he'd induce Kathleen's labor or perform a Caesarean, but he didn't think he'd be able to induce labor.

Sam spent the afternoon sitting beside Kathleen's bed. Casey had given her a light sedative, so she dozed and awakened, awakened and dozed, in the febrile light that came through the window and the cathode glare of a TV.

When visiting hours had ended, he kissed her and said goodbye.

He'd made it halfway to the door when she said, "Aren't you going to give me a goodbye kiss?"

"Sure."

He assumed she was still groggy from the sedative.

Sam kissed her again, lingeringly this time, so she'd remember, then he left the room. He went down the sickly beige hall past the nursery to the elevator, pushing the down button. He went through the lobby to the parking lot in front of the hospital. It was windy but clear, and he was sure you could count the stars if you had time.

As he came down the hill into the Smith Valley, he saw a small rabbit by the side of the highway. It looked as if it were paralyzed by the lights, by the passing cars, as if the big things of the world were too much for it.

Sam knew exactly how it felt.

By eight this morning I was in the X-ray lab, where a technician took two pictures of my pelvis. I always believed a pregnant woman couldn't be X-rayed, but I was wrong. It's only during the first 12 weeks of pregnancy, when an infant's bones and major organs are forming, that X-rays can be harmful or fatal to the baby.

Dr. Casey, in his green operating garb, stopped by my room to tell me he'd already seen the films and that he definitely couldn't induce labor.

He said, "The baby's head is too large to go down the birth canal, so I'm going to do a Caesarean. It has nothing to do with those old pelvic fractures."

After Casey left, a nurse brought in a huge vase filled with sunflowers. She was overweight and looked as if someone had stuffed her into her uniform, but her smile was as large as she was.

"Someone sure must love you," she said, then she put the vase on a table near the bed and handed me the card that had come with the flowers.

I didn't have to read it to know they were from Sam.

It was strange to awaken without her.

He lay in bed, watching the light gradually brighten as it came through the shutters, then he shaved and brushed his teeth before taking a shower. Then he made the bed, although he couldn't remember making one since he had spent a year at a military academy in San Rafael. He made it because it was something Kathleen would do.

He walked to Casino West, where he ordered coffee, a side of bacon and a side of home fries with green peppers and onions. He sat at a booth for two because it was where he and Kathleen had sat almost every morning when they'd moved to Yerington and because he'd become used to the waitress.

Belinda was a single mom with an eight year old boy and a one year old girl, and she always greeted you the same way. "How ya doin'?" She had long brown hair that was done up in a bun, and she had huge hips. He suspected she'd never read a book.

He finished breakfast, tipping her five dollars, then walked up Main Street, past a barbershop, a car dealership and a Mexican market. Someone wearing a suit and tie, carrying a briefcase, was going up the court house steps.

When he got home, the phone was ringing. He was sure it would be Kathleen, because almost no one phoned them, particularly early in the morning, so he said, "How are you?"

"Probably better than you are," she said.

That didn't seem improbable.

I'm surprised. My parents came to see me for a few hours yesterday afternoon. It was the first time I've been in a hospital when they didn't bring me a gift. When I was in a hospital with my third broken knee, my parents brought me flowers and candy, along with a tiny stuffed bear that was pale green, but they loved Clark.

This time my parents had to tolerate Sam, who was also here. My mother kept asking me how I felt, how did I really feel, and I kept saying, "I'm fine, mom, I'm all right," but she was sure anything I had to say that was positive must be a lie. All my father did was complain about how awful the weather had been when they'd crossed Donner Summit. It was snowing.

After everyone left, my roommate said she noticed my parents just talked to me and ignored Sam.

I said, "This was one of the good days. They didn't try to rip each other's throats out."

'Oh," she said, "why would they want to do that?"

"It's a long story," I said.

One of Sam's classmates had kicked the door to Sam's locker as he'd tried to pry it open when he was in the tenth grade. Sam stared at the blood spurting from his finger, as if it belonged to someone else, then he swung at the student who was silhouetted against a red background. (After that, Sam understood what people meant when they talked about "seeing red.") The student laughed and turned away, but Sam whirled him around, smashing his head against the handle of another locker. He was pounding the student's head against the concrete floor when the vice-principal pulled him off. Sam never wanted to get that angry again, but he was almost that furious after spending an afternoon with Kathleen's parents in an over-heated room that seemed too small, too confining, for so many people.

Welfare is paying for my roommate's baby, as well as the two year old Shelva left with her parents. She gave birth to Michael two days ago.

The nurses brought the babies to their mothers for their morning feeding today. I asked Shelva if I could hold her baby after he finished his bottle. Our contact only lasted a few minutes. Michael lay quietly in my arms, then yawned. I smiled and returned Michael to his mother.

By tomorrow morning I'll know what my baby's name will be. I wish Sam could be in the delivery room with me, since we completed all the natural childbirth classes, but they won't let him since I'm having a Caesarean. I hope Sam will let me name the baby Sara.

When he came to see me this morning, he asked how I felt, and I said, "Clean. I feel clean. I was allowed to take a shower this morning, and I even got to wash my hair," then I pointed to the windowsill. "Look at the carnations my parents sent."

Sam was sitting on a chair next to the bed, holding my hand, and I could feel his body stiffen. I was woozy from the darvon Casey had given me.

I remember Sam saying, "Don't ever confuse how I feel about your mother with how I feel about you," then I fell asleep.

He sat on a chair between the window overlooking the emergency entrance and Kathleen's bed, watching her sleep, the *I Love You* heart-shaped pillow she'd given him tucked against her chin. She'd told the nurses he'd given her the pillow because she wanted them to know how much he loved her, but the fabrication bothered him. He'd always prided himself on telling the truth, at least in his filmmaking, but he'd lied in most of his relationships with women, until he'd met Sara.

He spent eight hours a day here, all he was allowed, but didn't mind it, although he could think of places he'd rather be. But this was leading to something positive, hopeful, to new life.

Casey was going to perform the Caesarean tomorrow morning at 7:30. They'd discussed having him perform a ligation at the same time, but Kathleen could take the pill for another year or two without any bad side effects, so she was going to go back on it. Maybe they'd want a second child and there was always the chance that something bad could happen to this one, but they didn't dwell on that. He'd seen enough dying, enough death.

The top sheet on Kathleen's bed had yellow, green and red stripes, which delighted her. Neither of them expected to find them in a hospital. The sheets made the room seem more cheerful, less antiseptic.

Earlier that afternoon, an orderly had shaved Kathleen's pubic hair and discovered a mole she didn't know she had there. It was strange how you kept learning things about yourself. He'd been surprised to discover how much he detested Kathleen's mother, but even she didn't bother him now. He'd be friends with her if she'd let him. He doubted it would work out that way, but there was always hope.

Dr. Casey came in to see me early this evening. He stayed for twenty minutes, the longest since I've been here. Odd to know so little about someone who's going to cut me open tomorrow morning.

The operation itself doesn't bother me. It's the after effects, learning how to move again, I remember, the pain that takes your breath away.

I know Sam will be here, waiting. Maybe he'll see the baby before I do. It will depend on how heavily I'm sedated.

I tell the nurses I don't care what sex the baby is, that I just want it to have character, but I really want a girl.

December 29th

6:29 a.m.

She was in the bathroom when he'd arrived, shortly after six. Before Sam could see her, a nurse told him he had to leave so she could prep Kathleen.

He sat in a waiting room with an ancient TV set and two very bad reproductions of Van Gogh's paintings. At first he thought they were badly lithographed, but the colors might have been dulled from cigarette smoke.

It had been strange to get up in the dark. He got out of bed at four, but he'd awakened at three, sleeping sporadically, dozing.

Making coffee, he noticed the peanut seed Kathleen had been nurturing in yarn had sprouted.

7:01

He held Kathleen's hand.

"I feel like I'm going to die," she said.

7:22

Two nurses wheeled Kathleen down the hall. She was heavily sedated, not aware of much besides her contractions, which came every seven minutes now.

It was strange. In twenty minutes or so they'd be parents, and they still weren't sure if it would be a girl or a boy.

Two nights ago, when he was leaving, a nurse who'd recognized him asked why Kathleen wasn't in a private room, as if money answered everything.

Sometimes it did.

Sometimes it didn't.

He said Kathleen felt more comfortable when she wasn't alone, when she wasn't getting special treatment. It made her nervous, the way some fancy restaurants did. It had taken her weeks to get accustomed to his Cadillac. She'd been used to Plymouths, Fords.

He and the nurse had talked for two or three minutes, while Sam was waiting for an elevator. When he'd left, the nurse had gone into Kathleen's room, telling her how much "class" Sam had. Telling her how good looking she was. How intelligent both of them were.

They'd be great parents.

8:02

He went to the water fountain for a drink he didn't really want.

8:08

He was sweating under his arms, but his hands were cold. Then the sweat on his fingers dried, and he sweat some more.

8:11

Two nurses showed Sam his daughter and told him what he already knew. "She's beautiful."

"Thanks," he said, "thanks."

He didn't know what else to say. What else to do. Was there some kind of protocol you were supposed to follow?

He stood there dumbly: relieved, happy.

"When can I see Kathleen?" he said.

"Soon," one of the nurses told him, "soon. She's doing fine."

9:00

She was sitting up in bed, holding their daughter, when he went into the room.

"The nurses told me you got to see her before I did, at least before I remembered anything," Kathleen said, then she paused, watching him move toward her. He had never seen anyone more beautiful. He touched the two of them.

"Are we going to name her Sara?" Kathleen asked.

"Sara sounds perfect," he said.

A generous donation has been made to both the Gwendolyn Strong Foundation and the Families of Spinal Muscular Atrophy for each copy of this work sold by our friends at Stovetopcover.com

Our books are bound by commitment.

To learn more about our commitment to bringing
great books to market while helping good causes,
please visit us on the web at
http://www.milversteadpublishing.com

www.ingramcontent.com/pod-product-compliance
Lightning Source LLC
Chambersburg PA
CBHW031300060726
47590CB00003B/985